NEEDLE IN A TIMESTACK

These tales of the society we are
destined to live in will make your mind
stand on end. Their wit, wisdom and
ecric insight combine to produce
an explosion of wondering fear.
You'll find television news items that
have studio directors; nurses and
doctors with a bedside manner to send
you screaming, if you can still run;
in fact, Robert Silverberg applauds our
naïvety but thinks we should grow up
before it's too late.

Needle In a Timestack

ROBERT SILVERBERG

SPHERE BOOKS LIMITED LONDON

First published in the United States of America
by Ballantine Books Inc.

Copyright © 1966 Robert Silverberg

First Sphere Books edition, 1967

Africa—East: Thomas Nelson & Sons Ltd.
Africa—South: Thomas Nelson & Sons Ltd.
Africa—West: Thomas Nelson & Sons Ltd.
Australia: Thomas Nelson & Sons Ltd.
Bahamas: Calypso Distributors Ltd.
Belgium: Agence et Messageries de la Presse, S.A.
Canada: Thomas Nelson & Sons Ltd.
Denmark: Sven Gade
France: Librairie Hachette
Germany: Distropa Buchvertrieb
Greece: Hellenic Distribution Agency Ltd.
Holland: Van Ditmar
Hong Kong: Western Publications Distribution Agency (HK) Ltd.
Iraq: Dar Alaruba Universal Distribution Co.
Israel: Steimatzky's Agency Ltd.
Lebanon: International Publishers Representatives
Malaya: Marican & Sons (Malaysia) (Sdn) Berhad
Malta: Progress Press Co. Ltd.
New Zealand: Hodder & Stoughton Ltd.
Portugal: Electroliber Limitada
Spain: Comercial Atheneum, S.A.
Sweden: Importbokhandeln
Switzerland: Friedr. Daeniker
Thailand: The Pramuansarn Publishing House
Zambia: Kingstons (North) Ltd.

TRADE MARK

Text Printed in Great Britain by Hazell Watson & Viney Ltd
Aylesbury, Bucks

CONTENTS

THE PAIN PEDDLERS

The phone bleeped. Northrop nudged the cut-in switch and heard Maurillo say, "We got a gangrene, chief. They're amputating tonight."

Northrop's pulse quickened at the thought of action. "What's the tab?" he asked.

"Five thousand for all rights."

"Anesthetic?"

"Natch," Maurillo said. "I tried it the other way."

"What did you offer?"

"Ten. It was no go."

Northrop sighed. "I'll have to handle it myself, I guess. Where's the patient?"

"Clinton General. In the wards."

Northrop raised a heavy eyebrow and glowered into the screen. "In the *wards*?" he bellowed. "And you couldn't get them to agree?"

Maurillo seemed to shrink. "It was the relatives, chief. They were stubborn. The old man, he didn't seem to give a damn, but the relatives—"

"Okay. You stay there. I'm coming over to close the deal," Northrop snapped. He cut the phone out and pulled a couple of blank waiver forms out of his desk, just in case the relatives backed down. Gangrene was gangrene, but ten grand was ten grand. And business was business. The networks were yelling. He had to supply the goods or get out.

9

He thumbed the autosecretary. "I want my car ready in thirty seconds. South Street exit."

"Yes, Mr. Northrop."

"If anyone calls for me in the next half hour, record it. I'm going to Clinton General Hospital, but I don't want to be called there."

"Yes, Mr. Northrop."

"If Rayfield calls from the network office, tell him I'm getting him a dandy. Tell him—oh, hell, tell him I'll call him back in an hour. That's all."

"Yes. Mr. Northrop."

Northrop scowled at the machine and left his office. The gravshaft took him down forty stories in almost literally no time flat. His car was waiting, as ordered, a long sleek '08 Frontenac with bubble top. Bulletproof, of course. Network producers were vulnerable to crackpot attacks.

He sat back, nestling into the plush upholstery. The car asked him where he was going, and he answered.

"Let's have a pep pill," he said.

A pill rolled out of the dispenser in front of him. He gulped it down. *Maurillo, you make me sick,* he thought. *Why can't you close a deal without me? Just once?*

He made a mental note: Maurillo had to go. The organization couldn't tolerate inefficiency.

The hospital was an old one. It was housed in one of the vulgar green-glass architectural monstrosities so popular sixty years before, a tasteless slab-sided thing without character or grace.

The main door irised and Northrop stepped through. The familiar hospital smell hit his nostrils. Most people found it unpleasant, but not Northrop. For him it was the smell of dollars.

The hospital was so old that it still had nurses and orderlies. Oh, plenty of mechanicals skittered up and down the corridors, but here and there a middle-aged

10

nurse, smugly clinging to her tenure, pushed a tray of mush along, or a doddering orderly propelled a broom. In his early days on video Northrop had done a documentary on these living fossils of the hospital corridors. He had won an award for the film. He remembered it for its crosscuts from baggy-faced nurses to gleaming mechanicals, its vivid presentation of the inhumanity of the new hospitals. It was a long time since Northrop had done a documentary of that sort. A different kind of show was the order of the day now, ever since the intensifiers came in and telecasting medicine became an art.

A mechanical took him to Ward Seven. Maurillo was waiting there, a short, bouncy little man who wasn't bouncing much now. He knew he had fumbled. Maurillo grinned up at Northrop, a hollow grin, and said, "You sure made it fast, chief! "

"How long would it take for the competition to cut in?" Northrop countered. "Where's the patient?"

"Down by the end. You see where the curtain is? I had that put up. To get in good with the heirs. The relatives, I mean."

"Fill me in," Northrop said. "Who's in charge?"

"The oldest son, Harry. Watch out for him. Greedy."

"Who isn't?" Northrop sighed.

They were at the curtain now. Maurillo parted it. All through the long ward, patients were stirring. Potential subjects for taping, all of them, Northrop thought. The world was so full of different kinds of sickness—and one sickness fed on another.

He stepped through the curtain. There was a man in the bed, drawn and gaunt, his hollow face greenish, stubbly. A mechanical stood next to the bed, with an intravenous tube running across and under the covers.

The patient looked at least ninety. Knocking off ten years for the effects of illness still made him pretty old, Northrop thought.

11

He confronted the relatives.

There were eight of them. Five women, ranging from middle age down to teens. Three men, the oldest about fifty, the other two in their forties. Sons and nieces and grand-daughters, Northrop figured.

He said gravely, "I know what a terrible tragedy this must be for all of you. A man in the prime of his life—head of a happy family—" Northrop stared at the patient. "But I know he'll pull through. I can see the strength in him."

The oldest relative said, "I'm Harry Gardner. I'm his son. You're from the network?"

"I'm the producer," Northrop said. "I don't ordinarily come in person, but my assistant told me what a great human situation there was here, what a brave person your father was—"

The man in the bed slept on. He looked bad.

Harry Gardner said, "We made an arrangement. Five thousand bucks. We wouldn't do it, except for the hospital bills. They can really wreck you."

"I understand perfectly," Northrop said in his most unctuous tones. "That's why we're prepared to raise our offer. We're well aware of the disastrous effects of hospit-alization on a small family, even today, in these times of protection. And so we can offer—"

"No! There's got to be anesthetic!" It was one of the daughters, a round, drab woman with colorless thin lips. "We ain't going to let you make him suffer!"

Northrop smiled. "It would only be a moment of pain for him. Believe me. We'd begin the anesthesia immedi-ately after the amputation. Just let us capture that single instant of—"

"It ain't right! He's old, he's got to be given the best treatment! The pain could kill him!"

"On the contrary," Northrop said blandly. "Scientific research has shown that pain is often beneficial in ampu-tation cases. It creates a nerve block, you see, that causes a kind of anesthesia of its own, without the harmful side effects of chemotherapy. And once the danger vectors are controlled, the normal anesthetic procedures can be invoked, and—" he took a deep breath, and went rolling glibly on to the crusher—"with the extra fee we'll provide, you can give your dear one the absolute finest in medical care. There'll be no reason to stint."

Wary glances were exchanged. Harry Gardner said, "How much are you offering for this absolute finest in medical care?"

"May I see the leg?" Northrop answered.

The coverlet was peeled back. Northrop stared.

It was a nasty case. Northrop was no doctor, but he had been in this line of work for five years, and that was long enough to give him an amateur acquaintance with disease. He knew the old man was in bad shape. It looked as though there had been a severe burn, high up along the calf, which had probably been treated only with first aid. Then, in happy proletarian ignorance, the family had let the old man rot until he was gangrenous. Now the leg was blackened, glossy, and swollen from mid-calf to the ends of the toes. Everything looked soft and decayed. Northrop had the feeling that he could reach out and break the puffy toes off, one at a time.

The patient wasn't going to survive.

Amputation or not, he was rotten to the core by this time. If the shock of amputation didn't do him in, general debilitation would. It was a good prospect for the show. It was the kind of stomach-turning vicarious suffering that millions of viewers gobbled up avidly.

Northrop looked up and said, "Fifteen thousand if you'll allow a network-approved surgeon to amputate under our conditions. And we'll pay the surgeon's fee besides."

"Well—"

"And we'll also underwrite the entire cost of postoperative care for your father," Northrop added smoothly.

13

"Even if he stays in the hospital for six months, we'll pay every nickel, over and above the telecast fee."

He had them. He could see the greed shining in their eyes. They were faced with bankruptcy. He had come to rescue them; and did it matter all that much if the old man didn't have anesthetic when they sawed his leg off? Why, he was hardly conscious even now. He wouldn't really feel a thing. Not really.

Northrop produced the documents, the waivers, the contracts covering residuals and Latin-American reruns, the payment vouchers, all the paraphernalia. He sent Maurillo scuttling off for a secretary, and a few moments later a glistening mechanical was taking it all down.

"If you'll put your name here, Mr. Gardner—"

Northrop handed the pen to the eldest son. Signed, sealed, delivered.

"We'll operate tonight," Northrop said. "I'll send our surgeon over immediately. One of our best men. We'll give your father the care he deserves."

He pocketed the documents.

It was done. Maybe it was barbaric to operate on an old man that way, Northrop thought. But he didn't bear the responsibility, after all. He was just giving the public what it wanted. What the public wanted was spouting blood and tortured nerves.

And what did it matter to the old man, really? Any experienced medic could tell you he was as good as dead. The operation wouldn't save him. Anesthesia wouldn't save him. If the gangrene didn't get him, postoperative shock would do him in. At worst, he would suffer only a few minutes under the knife . . . but at least his family would be free from the fear of financial ruin.

On the way out, Maurillo said, "Don't you think it's a little risky, chief? Offering to pay the hospitalization expenses, I mean?"

14

"You've got to gamble a little sometimes to get what you want," Northrop said.

"Yeah, but that could run to fifty, sixty thousand! What'll that do to the budget?"

Northrop grinned. "We'll survive. Which is more than the old man will. He can't make it through the night. We haven't risked a penny, Maurillo. Not a stinking cent."

Returning to the office, Northrop turned the papers on the Gardner amputation over to his assistants, set the wheels in motion for the show and prepared to call it a day.

There was only one bit of dirty work left to do. He had to fire Maurillo.

It wasn't called firing, of course. Maurillo had tenure, just like the hospital orderlies and everyone else below executive rank. It would have to be more a kick upstairs than anything else.

Northrop had been increasingly dissatisfied with the little man's work for months now. Today had been the clincher. Maurillo had no imagination. He didn't know how to close a deal. Why hadn't he thought of underwriting the hospitalization? *If I can't delegate responsibility to him*, Northrop told himself, *I can't use him at all*. There were plenty of other assistant producers in the outfit who'd be glad to step in.

Northrop spoke to a couple of them. He made his choice: A young fellow named Barton, who'd been working on documentaries all year. Barton had done the plane-crash deal in London in the spring. He had a fine touch for the gruesome. He had been on hand at the World's Fair fire last year at Juneau. Yes, Barton was the man.

The next part was the sticky one. Things could go wrong.

Northrop phoned Maurillo, even though Maurillo was only two rooms away—these things were never done in

15

person—and said, "I've got some good news for you, Ted. We're shifting you to a new program."

"Shifting—?"

"That's right. We had a talk in here this afternoon, and we decided you were being wasted on the blood-and-guts show. You need more scope for your talents. So we're moving you over to *Kiddie Time*. We think you'll really blossom there. You and Sam Kline and Ed Bragan ought to make a terrific team."

Northrop saw Maurillo's pudgy face crumble. The arithmetic was getting home; over here, Maurillo was Number Two, and on the new show, a much less important one, he'd be Number Three. The pay meant nothing, of course; didn't Internal Revenue take it all anyway? It was a thumping boot, and Maurillo knew it.

The mores of the situation called for Maurillo to pretend he was receiving a rare honor. He didn't play the game. He squinted and said, "Just because I didn't sign up that old man's amputation?"

"What makes you think—"

"Three years I've been with you! Three years, and you kick me out just like that!"

"I told you, Ted, we thought this would be a big opportunity for you. It's a step up the ladder. It's—"

Maurillo's fleshy face puffed up with rage. "It's getting junked," he said bitterly. "Well, never mind, huh? It so happens I've got another offer. I'm quitting before you can can me. You can take your tenure and—"

Northrop hastily blanked the screen.

The idiot, he thought. *The fat little idiot. Well, to hell with him!*

He cleared his desk, and cleared his mind of Ted Maurillo and his problems. Life was real, life was earnest. Maurillo just couldn't take the pace, that was all.

Northrop prepared to go home. It had been a long day.

At eight that evening came word that old Gardner was about to undergo the amputation. At ten, Northrop was phoned by the network's own head surgeon, Dr. Steele, with the news that the operation had failed.

"We lost him," Steele said in a flat, unconcerned voice. "We did our best, but he was a mess. Fibrillation set in, and his heart just ran away. Not a damned thing we could do."

"Did the leg come off?"

"Oh, sure. All this was after the operation."

"Did it get taped?"

"Processing it now."

"Okay," Northrop said. "Thanks for calling."

"Sorry about the patient."

"Don't worry yourself," Northrop said. "It happens to the best of us."

The next morning, Northrop had a look at the rushes. The screening was in the 23rd Floor studio, and a select audience was on hand—Northrop, his new assistant producer Barton, a handful of network executives, a couple of men from the cutting room. Slick, bosomy girls handed out intensifier helmets. No mechanicals doing the work here!

Northrop slipped the helmet on over his head. He felt the familiar surge of excitement as the electrodes descended and contact was made. He closed his eyes. There was a thrum of power somewhere in the room as the EEG-amplifier went into action. The screen brightened.

There was the old man. There was the gangrenous leg. There was Dr. Steele, crisp and rugged and dimple-chinned, the network's star surgeon, $250,000 a year's worth of talent. There was the scalpel, gleaming in Steele's hand.

Northrop began to sweat. The amplified brain waves were coming through the intensifier, and he felt the throbbing in the old man's leg, felt the dull haze of pain behind the old man's forehead, felt the weakness of being eighty years old and half dead.

Steele was checking out the electronic scalpel, now, while the nurses fussed around, preparing the man for the amputation. In the finished tape, there would be music, narration, all the trimmings, but now there was just a soundless series of images, and, of course, the tapped brain waves of the sick man.

The leg was bare.

The scalpel descended.

Northrop winced as vicarious agony shot through him. He could feel the blazing pain, the brief searing hell as the scalpel slashed through diseased flesh and rotting bone. His whole body trembled, and he bit down hard on his lips and clenched his fists, and then it was over.

There was a cessation of pain. A catharsis. The leg no longer sent its pulsating messages to the weary brain. Now there was shock, the anesthesia of hyped-up pain, and with the shock came calmness. Steele went about the mop-up operation. He tidied the stump, bound it.

The rushes flickered out in anticlimax. Later, the production crew would tie up the program with interviews of the family, perhaps a shot of the funeral, a few observations on the problem of gangrene in the aged. Those things were the extras. What counted, what the viewers wanted, was the sheer nastiness of vicarious pain, and that they got in full measure. It was a gladiatorial contest without the gladiators, masochism concealed as medicine. It worked. It pulled in the viewers by the million.

Northrop patted sweat from his forehead.

"Looks like we got ourselves quite a little show here, boys," he said in satisfaction.

The mood of satisfaction was still on him as he left the building that day. All day he had worked hard, getting

18

the show into its final shape, cutting and polishing. He enjoyed the element of craftsmanship. It helped him to forget some of the sordidness of the program.

Night had fallen when he left. He stepped out of the main entrance and a figure strode forward, a bulky figure, medium height, tired face. A hand reached out, thrusting him roughly back into the lobby of the building.

At first Northrop didn't recognize the face of the man. It was a blank face, a nothing face, a middle-aged empty face. Then he placed it.

Harry Gardner. The son of the dead man.

"Murderer!" Gardner shrilled. "You killed him! He would have lived if you'd used anesthetics! You phony, you murdered him so people would have thrills on television!"

Northrop glanced up the lobby. Someone was coming, around the bend. Northrop felt calm. He could stare this nobody down until he fled in fear.

"Listen," Northrop said, "we did the best medical science can do for your father. We gave him the ultimate in scientific care. We—"

"You murdered him!"

"No," Northrop said, and then he said no more, because he saw the sudden flicker of a slice gun in the blank-faced man's fat hand.

He backed away. But it didn't help, because Gardner punched the trigger and an incandescent bolt flared out, and sliced across Northrop's belly just as efficiently as the surgeon's scalpel had cut through the gangrenous leg.

Gardner raced away, feet clattering on the marble floor. Northrop dropped, clutching himself.

His suit was seared. There was a slash through his abdomen, a burn an eighth of an inch wide and perhaps four inches deep, cutting through intestines, through organs, through flesh. The pain hadn't begun yet. His

19

nerves weren't getting the message through to his stunned brain.

But then they were; and Northrop coiled and twisted in agony that was anything but vicarious now.

Footsteps approached.

"Jeez," a voice said.

Northrop forced an eye open. Maurillo. Of all people, Maurillo.

"A doctor," Northrop wheezed. "Fast! Christ, the pain! Help me, Ted!"

Maurillo looked down, and smiled. Without a word, he stepped to the telephone booth six feet away, dropped in a token, punched out a call.

"Get a van over here, fast. I've got a subject, chief."

Northrop writhed in torment. Maurillo crouched next to him. "A doctor," Northrop murmured. "A needle, at least. Gimme a needle! The pain—"

"You want me to kill the pain?" Maurillo laughed. "Nothing doing. You just hang on. You stay alive till we get that hat on your head and tape the whole thing."

"But you don't work for me. You're off the program—"

"Sure," Maurillo said. "I'm with Transcontinental now. They're starting a blood-and-guts show too. Only they don't need waivers."

Northrop gaped, Transcontinental? That bootleg outfit that peddled tapes in Afghanistan and Mexico and Ghana and God knew where else? Not even a network show, he thought. No fee! Dying in agony for the benefit of a bunch of lousy tapeleggers. That was the worst part, Northrop thought. Only Maurillo would pull a deal like that.

"A needle! For God's sake, Maurillo, a needle!"

"Nothing doing. The van'll be here any minute. They'll sew you up, and we'll tape it nice."

Northrop closed his eyes. He felt the coiling intestines

20

blazing within him. He willed himself to die, to cheat Maurillo.

But it was no use. He remained alive and suffering.

He lived for an hour. That was plenty of time to tape his dying agonies. The last thought he had was that it was a damned shame he couldn't star on his own show.

PASSPORT TO SIRIUS

Consumer Sixth Class David Carman watched the yellow snake that was the morning telefax sheet come rippling from the wall slot of his bachelor flat. The folds of plastic-impregnated tape slithered into the receiving tray, and Carman surveyed them glumly. He knew there would only be more bad news—more tales of defeat in the Sirian war, more heralding of price increases on the consumer front.

After a moment of hesitation Carman gathered up the telefax spool and slipped it into the scanner-reader. He shuddered as the first news appeared on the screen.

COSTLY SETBACK IN SIRIUS

War Sector, 14 Nov (via subradio)—A Sirian pitchfork maneuver hurled Earth lines back today in the battle for Sirius IV. The sudden alien thrust cost Earth eight destroyers and more than a hundred casualties.

The push began, according to a front-lines communique, when eleven Sirian battle cruisers initiated diversionary tactics in orbit around the Earth base on Sirius IV's seventh moon. Bringing in a battalion of mosquito ships next, the aliens successfully—

Morosely Carman thumbed his weary eyes and moved the scanner further along. All these war stories were pretty much alike, he thought. And the telefax reveled in detailed descriptions of each offensive and defensive tactic. Carman knew nothing of war-making; the details bored him.

But the next item was hardly more cheering.

PRICE INDEX TO JUMP AGAIN

Lower Urb-district, 16 Nov—Consumer prices are due for another increased spiral as a result of the severe setback suffered by Terran forces in the Sirian sector. Economic Regulator Harrison Morch revealed this morning that a down-the-line 5% increase is likely.

"We tried to hold the line," commented Regulator Morch. "The inflationary trend was too strong to buck, however. It is to be hoped that conclusion of hostilities will soon bring about a reversion to peacetime living standards and—"

With an angry, impatient gesture, Carman blanked the screen. There was little sense spending good money subscribing to the 'fax service if it only brought bad news.

Things hadn't been this bad a year ago, before the war started, he thought, as he dialed breakfast and took his seat by the dispensall. He had even been thinking of applying for a marriage permit, then. Now, of course, it was out of the question; his economic status was totally altered. And Sally, who worked for the Bureau of Extraterrestrial Affairs, had received a pay boost that put her entirely beyond Carman's aspirations. She was Third Class, now, and would soon marry a wealthy bureau official.

Carman broodingly munched his somewhat dry algae omelet. He was thirty-three, and not getting younger. He was too pale, too thin, his eyes too close-set, his hair growing sparse. And it seemed that whenever he got some money saved and looked around to better his position, along came some war to send prices shooting up and cripple his savings. Five years ago there had been that thing in Procyon, and then a year or two of peace followed by a scuffle out near Proxima Centauri. And now Sirius.

You can't win, he thought. He finished breakfast mechanically, dropped the dishes in the disposall, and selected his second-best suit with a quick, bitter jab at the wardrobe control buttons.

It came issuing forth: gray crepe, with dark blue trim. The jacket was getting tattered at the elbows.

I'd better buy a new suit, Carman decided, as he stepped out on the pickup platform to hail a jet-cab. *Before clothing prices get astronomical.*

He reached the office at 0700 that morning, with dawn barely brightening the late autumn sky. Carman worked as a porter in the permit-processing department of the Confederation Passport Office, and so as a government employee had little recourse when the periodic inflation spirals came; he could hardly go on strike against the Confederation.

A good-sized batch of passport applications had already accumulated at his receiving tray. Carman slid easily into the seat, flashed bright but hollow smiles at the five or six fellow workers nearest him, and grabbed at the top sheet of the stack. He estimated quickly that 180 applications had arrived so far. They would be pouring in at a rate of seven a minute the rest of the day.

He computed:

If I process one form every six seconds, ten a minute, I'll gain three per minute on them. Which means I'll catch up with them in about an hour.

If he kept up the ten-a-minute pace, he'd be free to take short breathers later on. This was one of the games he played to make his dreary work more palatable.

The first application was from Consumer Second Class

Leebig D. Quellen and family; Consumer Second Class Quellen wanted to visit the Ganymede outpost next summer. Carman plunged the application into the bin stencil-labelled *14a* with his left hand, and with his right took another from the waiting stack. Sort with the left, grab with the right. Carman swayed rhythmically in his seat as he fell into the pattern of the day's work.

After a while he began hitting them twelve to a minute, sometimes thirteen. By 0757 his tray was empty. He sighed. Eight seconds of free time, now, until the next permit reared its ugly head.

Sort, grab . . . sort, grab . . . it was dull but essentially simple work, in a mechanical way. It scarcely taxed his brain. But he was paid accordingly. $163 a week, barely a subsistence wage before the last spiral. And now—

1030 came. Break time. Carman stretched and rose, noticing angrily that the girl in the upstairs receiving room had slipped three applications in after break time sounded. She was always pulling tricks like that.

Carman had long since reduced break time to a ritual. He crossed the office to the cleanall and held his hands in the energizing bath until his fingertips were wiped clean of the accumulation of stylus grime; then he glanced out the single big window at the crowded city, turned, and smiled at Montano, the heavy-set fellow who had occupied the next desk for the six years Carman had worked for the Passport Office.

"Nice day," Montano said. "For November."

"Yes."

"See the morning 'fax? Looks like another upping for prices."

Carman nodded unhappily. "I saw. Don't know how we'll manage."

"Oh, we'll get along. We always do. The wife's due for a raise soon anyway." Montano's wife pushed buttons in a car autofactory. Somehow she seemed to be due for a raise almost every other week.

"That's nice," Carman said.

"Yeah."

"Does she think cars are going up?"

"Damn right," Montano said. "Ford-Chrysler's boosting the stock model to six thousand next month. Need turbo-generators for the war effort, they say. We already got our order in at the old price. You better buy fast if you want one, Carman. Save five hundred bucks now if you're smart."

"I don't need a new car," Carman said.

"Better get *anything* you need now, anyways. Every thing's going up. Always does, wartime."

The bell tone announced the end of break time. Carman reached his desk just in time to see a passport application come fluttering down, followed seconds later by another.

"Demons take that girl," he muttered softly. She always cut her break short to plague him with extra work. Now she was six—no, seven—ahead of him.

Justin C. Froelich and family, of Minnetonka, wished permission to visit Pluto next July. Wearily, Carman dropped Justin C. Froelich's application in the proper bin, and reached for the next.

He was seething inwardly, cursing the Passport Office, the girl upstairs, inflation, Economic Regulator Morch, and the world in general. It seemed to be a rat-race with no exit from the treadmill.

I've been pushed around too long, he thought. I ought to fight back a little. Somehow.

Consumer Sixth Class Carman was on the verge of changing the course of his life. An hour more passed, and 193 additional passport applications disappeared into bins. Finally, he made up his mind to act.

The recruiting officer was a spade-faced, dark-complex-

26

ioned man with angular features and bright white teeth. He wore the green-and-gold uniform of the United Military Services of Earth. He stared levelly across his shining bare desk at Carman and said, "Would you mind repeating that?"

"I said I wanted to fight. Against Sirius."

The recruiting officer frowned ponderously. After a long pause he said, "I don't see how I can guarantee that. We enroll you; the computer ships you out. Whether you get sent to the war zone or not depends on a variable complex of factors which certainly no civilian should be expected to understand." He shoved a form across the desk toward Carman. "If you'll fill this out, Mac, we can—"

"No," Carman said. "I want a guarantee that I'll see action in the Sirius sector. Dammit, Lieutenant—"

"Sergeant."

"—Sergeant, I'm thirty-three. I'm as close to being nobody as anybody can get. If I'm lucky I'll get as high as Third Class someday. I've saved ten thousand bucks, and I supppose the new inflation's going to knock my savings in half the way the last one did."

"Mr. Carman, I don't see how all this—"

"You will. For thirty-three years I've been sitting around on the home front going up and down with each economic spiral while Earth fights wars in Procyon and Proxima C and half a dozen other places. I'm tired of staying home. I want to enlist."

"Sure, Mac, but—"

"But I don't want to enlist just to wear a uniform and police the frontiers on Betelgeuse. I want to go to Sirius, and I want to fight. Once in my life I want to engage in positive action on behalf of a Cause." Carman took a deep breath; he hadn't spoken this many words in succession in a long, long time. "Do you understand now? Will you guarantee that I'll be shipped to Sirius if I sign up?"

The sergeant exhaled deeply, unhappily. "I've explained twice that the matter's not in my hands. Maybe I could attach a recommendation—"

"A *guarantee*."

"But—" A crafty light appeared in the recruiting sergeant's eyes; he drummed the desktop momentarily and said, "You're a very persistent man, Mac. You win; I'll see you get assigned to the war zone. Now, why don't you just sign your name here—"

Carman shook his head. "No thanks. I just changed my mind."

Before the sergeant could protest, Carman had backed warily out of the office and was gone. It had abruptly occurred to him that a recruiting officer's promise was not necessarily final. And there were more direct methods he could use to get into the war.

He returned to the Passport Office at 1313, and the robot eye at the office door took note of it, clicking loudly as he passed through. Ordinarily Carman would have groaned at the loss of thirteen minutes' pay, but, then ordinarily he would have been at his desk promptly at 1300 anyway.

Everyone else was busily at work; heads bowed, hands groping madly for the incoming applications, his fellow sorters presented an oddly ludicrous sight. Carman resumed his place. Nearly a hundred waiting permits had stacked themselves in the receiving tray during his absence—but this, too, hardly troubled him now.

He went through them at a frantic pace, occasionally hitting as high as twenty per minute. Plenty of them were going to the wrong bins, he realized, but this was no time to worry about that. He caught up with the posting department in less than forty minutes, and made use of his first eight-second breather to draw a blank passport application from his desk drawer; he had always kept a few on hand there.

28

He filled out the blank patiently, in eight-second bursts between each of the arrivals from above. Where it said *Name and Status,* he wrote *Consumer Sixth Class David Carman.* Where it said *Intended Destination,* he inscribed *Sirius VII* in tidy cursives. Sirius VII was outside the war zone, and so theoretically within reach of commercial traffic, but passports to anywhere in the Sirius system were granted only by special dispensation since the outbreak of hostilities, and Carman knew he had small chance of receiving such dispensation.

Which was why, after the form was completely filled out, he thoughtfully scribbled an expert forgery of the Secretary of Extraterrestrial Affairs' signature on the bottom of the sheet, okaying the application. Humming gently, he dropped the completed blank into the bin labeled *82g* and returned his attention to the labors of the day.

The passport took eight days to come through. Carman had some uneasy moments while waiting, though he was ultimately confident of success. After all, the workers who processed the sorted applications and issued the passports probably handled their work as mechanically and hastily as he did in the level above them—and he never had time to check for possible forgeries, so why should they? Never-ending cascades of passport applications descended on them; probably they cursed him for working so fast, just as he in turn scowled up the chute at the girl in the top level.

Five seconds after the passport to Sirius dropped out of his mail chute, Carman was on the phone talking to the secretary of the Personnel Chief at the Passport Office.

"Yes, I said Carman. David Carman, Sixth Class. I've enlisted in the Services and my resignation is effective today. Yes, *today.* My pay check? Oh, burn it," Carman said impatiently, and hung up. So much for past associations.

29

Carman withdrew his entire savings—$9,783.61. The roboteller handed over the cash without comment. Carman took the thick pile of crisp bills, counted slowly through them to the great annoyance of the people behind him in line, and nudged the *acknowledge* stud to let the teller know the transaction was complete. Outside the bank, he signaled for another copter and took it to the Upper Urbdistrict Spaceport, far out on what had once been Long Island.

"A ticket to Sirius?" the dispatcher asked, after the robot ticket vendor had passed Carman on to him in perplexity. "But the war, you know—we've curtailed our service to that entire sector."

"I don't care," Carman said stolidly. He was growing accustomed to being forceful now; it came easily to him, and he enjoyed it. "You advertise through transportation to Sirius VII. I've got a passport that says I can go there, and I've got six thousand dollars to pay my way. Cash."

"This is very irregular," moaned the dispatcher, a short harried-looking little man. "We discontinued passenger service to that system eight months ago, when—"

"You could lose your franchise for this," Carman snapped bluntly. "Sirius VII is nonbelligerent. I have money and a passport. I demand transportation."

In the end, they diverted a freight run bound for Deneb, and put Carman aboard with the promise that they'd drop him at Sirius VII. His passport was in order, and he had the cash for the payment.

The trip took three weeks of steady hyperdrive travel. Six other humans were on board, all bad-smelling crewmen, and the crew of a space freighter is hardly pleasant company on a three-week journey. Carman kept to himself, inventing a form of solitaire he could play making use of the hundred-dollar bills, of which he had more than thirty left even after paying passage. The ship's cargo consisted of steers slated for an agrarian colony orbiting Deneb, and Carman lived in a cramped cabin just aft of the cargo hold. He got little sleep.

They put him down finally on the concrete landing apron at Zuorf, crown city of Sirius VII, on the fifth day of 2672, having first radioed the Terran consul there to let them know he was coming. Biggest and muggiest of the twelve planets that circled the dog star, Sirius VII was a vast mountainous world with ugly sprawling cities crammed between the jagged peaks; its people were brawny ursinoids, not long escaped from their neolithic culture stage.

As it happened, some sort of local celebration was in full sway when Carman, a solitary figure with a solitary suitcase of belongings, left the spaceport. Great heavy-set creatures were whirling up and down the streets in each other's arms, looking like so many dancing bears clad in tinsel and frills. Carman stepped hastily back into the shadow of a squat yellow-painted building while a platoon of the huge shaggy aliens came thundering past, to the gay accompaniment of distant tootling music composed in excruciating quarter-tone intervals.

A hand fell lightly on his shoulder. Carman turned and jumped away all in the same nervous motion. He saw an Earthman behind him, clad in the somber black vestments of the Terran diplomatic corps.

"Pardon me if I startled you," the stranger said in a soft, cultured voice. He was a neatly turned out, mildly foppish-looking man in his forties, with elegant features, well-groomed dark hair, delicately shaven brow ridges. Only the startling brass ring through his nostrils marred his otherwise distinguished upper-class appearance.

"I'm the Terran consul on this world," he went on, in the same gentle tones. "Adrian Blyde's my name. Am I right in assuming you're the man who has just dropped off by that freighter?"

31

"You are. I'm David Carman of Earth. Want to see my passport?"

Consul Blyde smiled serenely. "In due time, Mr. Carman. I'm sure it's in good order. But would you mind telling me precisely *why* you've come to Sirius VII?"

"To join the armed forces. I want to take part in the Sirian campaign."

"To join the armed forces," Blyde repeated in a faintly wonderstruck voice. "Well well well. That's very interesting, Mr. Carman. Very. Would you come this way, please?"

Blyde seized him firmly by the fleshy part of his arm and propelled him across the wide, poorly paved street, between two pairs of madly careening bearlike beings, and into a narrow doorway in a building constructed of purple brick.

"The autochthones are celebrating their annual fertility dance through the city from morning to night without rest. Those that keep on their feet the whole day without collapsing are entitled to mate. The weak ones have to try again next year. It's quite a neat genetic system, really."

Carman glanced back through the doorway at the hordes of spinning aliens weaving wildly down the broad street, locked an office door and gestured within to a cluttered

"The nose rings denote masculinity," Blyde said. "Terran males who stay here have to wear them too; the natives are very, very fussy about that. When in Rome, you know. I'll give you yours tonight."

"Just a minute," Carman said worriedly, as Blyde unlocked an office door and gestured within to a cluttered little room lined with booktapes and scattered papers. "I don't plan to stay here, you know. The military action's on Sirius IV. That's where I'm going as soon as I've seen the authorities and enlisted."

Blyde dropped heavily into a well-upholstered pneumochair, wiped perspiration from his brow with an obviously scented cloth, and sighed unhappily. "My dear Mr. Carman: I don't know what motives impelled you to come to this system, nor by what chicanery you wangled your passage. But now that you're here, there are several things you should know."

"Such as?"

"For one, there are no hostilities currently taking place anywhere in the Sirius System."

Stunned, Carman gasped, "No—hostilities? Then the war's over?"

Blyde touched his fingertips lightly together. "You misunderstand. There never *was* any war between Earth and Sirius IV. Care for a drink?"

"Rye," Carman said automatically. "Never—was—a—war? But—how—"

"Economic Regulator Harrison Morch of Earth is a great man," Blyde said with seeming irrelevancy, putting his head back as if studying the reticulated pattern of paint cracks on the office ceiling. An air conditioner hummed ineffectually somewhere. "Economic Regulator Morch has devoted a lifetime of study to examining the motives govering fluctuations in economic trends."

Carman's throat felt terribly dry. The moist warmth of Sirius VII's atmosphere, the additional drag of the heavier gravity, the calm blandness of the consul's manner, the sheer nonsense he was talking—all these factors were combining to make Carman thoroughly sick.

"What does all this have to do with—"

Blyde raised one manicured hand. "Economic Regulator Morch, through his studies, has reduced to a formula the general economic principle known to theorists for centuries—that spending increases in direct proportion to adverse military news. Consumers go on buying sprees, remembering the last cycle of shortages and of rapid price increases. Money flows more freely. Of course, when the war situation lasts long enough, a period of inflation

33

sets in—making it necessary that an equally virulent peace be waged."

Dimly Carman sensed what was coming. "No," he said.

"Yes. There is no war with Sirius. It was a stroke of genius on Economic Regulator Morch's part to take advantage of the uncertainty of interstellar communication to enforce a news block on the entire Sirius system. It's a simple matter to distribute fabricated war communiques, invent wholly fictitious spaceships which perish gorily on the demand of the moment, arouse public interest and keep it at a high pitch—"

"You mean," Carman said tonelessly, "that Morch invented this whole war, and arranges Terran victories and losses to fit economic conditions back home?"

"It is a brilliant plan," said Blyde, smiling complacently. "If a decline in spending occurs, word of severe losses in space reaches the home front, and the bad news serves to unloose the purse strings. When the economy has been reinflated, Earth's legions forge on to victory, and spending drops off again. We spend heavily in times of stress, when we need consolation—not in peacetime."

Carman blinked. "I spent six thousand dollars and forged a passport to come here and find out *this!* The one time in my life I decided to *do* something, instead of sitting back and letting things happen to me, I discover it's all a hoax," He flexed his fingers experimentally, as if wondering what he might do with them.

Blyde seemed to be sympathetic. "It is, I realize, terribly awkward for you. But no more so than it is to us, who have the strenuous task of preserving this beneficial hoax and protecting it from would-be exposers."

"Are you going to kill me, then?"

Blyde blanched at the blunt question. "Mr. Carman! We are not barbarians!"

"Well, what *are* you going to do with me?"

The consul shrugged. "The one completely satisfactory

34

thing. We'll find you a good job here on Sirius VII. You'll be much happier here than you ever were on Earth. Naturally, you can't be permitted to return home."

But the man who can forge a passport to Sirius can also find a way home. In Carman's case it took him seven full months—months of living in the sticky endless heat of Sirius VII, dodging the playful ursinoid natives, kowtowing to Blyde (whose secretary he became, at $60 a week) and wearing a brass nose ring through his nostrils.

It was seven months before he had mastered Blyde's signature to his own satisfaction, and knew enough of local diplomatic protocol to be able to requisition a spaceship from the small military outpost just outside Zuorf. A messenger—there were no phones on the planet, for obscure religious reasons—came to the Consulate to announce that the ship was ready.

"Wait outside," Carman told the boy.

Blyde looked up from behind his desk and said, "What ship does he mean?"

"The one I'm taking back to Earth," said Carman, and released the sleep capsule. Blyde smiled sweetly as he slipped into unconsciousness. Carman followed the boy to the spaceport.

A slim, trim two-man ship waited there, sleek and golden-hulled in the bright sunlight. The pilot was an efficient looking space-tanned man named Duane.

"Diplomatic pouch," Carman said, handing over the leather attaché case he had prepared for the occasion. Duane stored it reverently in the hold, and they blasted off.

"Sirius IV first," Carman ordered. "I'm supposed to take films. Top secret, of course."

"Of course."

They circled the small pockmarked gray fourth planet at 50,000 feet, and Carman took enough cloud-piercing infrared shots to prove conclusively that there was not and never had been any war between the amiable amphibious aborigines and Earth. Satisfied, he ordered the pilot to proceed immediately toward Sol.

They reached Earth nineteen days later, on 3 August 2672. A squad of security police was waiting for them as they landed at Upper Urbdistrict Spaceport, and Carman was swiftly conveyed to a cell in Confederation Detention House in the tunnels far below Old Manhattan. Blyde had sent word ahead via subradio concerning Carman's escape, it seemed.

In his cell, later that evening Carman was visited by a parched-looking, almost fleshless man in the blue cape and red wig of high governmental office.

"So you're the culprit! "

"That's what they tell me. Who are you?"

"Ferdan Veller, Administrative Assistant to Regulator Morch. The Regulator sent me to see who you were and what you were like."

"Well, now you've seen," Carman said. "Get out."

Assistant Veller's melancholy eyes widened. "I see you're a forceful man, Mr. Carman. No doubt you're full of plans for escaping, recapturing your confiscated films, and letting the world know what a dastardly hoax is being perpetrated in the interests of a balanced economy. Eh?"

"I might be," Carman admitted.

"You might be interested in this morning's telefax sheet, then," Veller said. He extended a torn-off yellow strip.

The headline was:

NEW AGGRESSION
THREATENS EARTH!

Government City, 3 Aug 2672—Word reached Earth today of yet another threat to her peace, coming hot on the heels of the recently concluded police action in the Sirius sector. Forces in the Great Andromeda Nebula have issued statements inimical to Earth, and a new conflict looms—"

"You killed off Sirius because you were afraid I'd expose it," Carman said accusingly. "And now you're starting up a new one."

Veller nodded smugly. "Quite. The Great Andromeda Nebula happens to be 900,000 light years away. The round trip, even by hyperdrive, takes some twenty years." He grinned, showing a double row of square tartared teeth. "You're a forceful man, Mr. Carman. You may very well escape. You may even reach Andromeda and return with evidence once again unmasking us. If you live long enough to return, that is. I think our economic program is in no immediate danger from you."

He left, smiling gravely. The cell door closed with a harsh metallic crash.

"Come back!" Carman yelled. "You can't hoax mankind like that! I'll let everyone know! I'll get out and expose—"

There was no answer, not even a catcall. No one was listening. And, Carman realized dully, no one was going to listen to him at all, ever again.

BIRDS OF A FEATHER

It was our first day of recruiting on the planet, and the alien life forms had lined up for hundreds of feet back from my rented office. As I came down the block from the hotel, I could hear and see and smell them with ease.

My three staff men, Auchinleck, Stebbins and Ludlow, walked shieldwise in front of me. I peered between them to size up the crop. The aliens came in every shape and form, in all colours and textures—and all of them eager for a Corrigan contract. The Galaxy is full of bizarre beings, but there's barely a species anywhere that can resist the old exhibitionist urge.

"Send them in one at a time," I told Stebbins. I ducked into the office, took my place back of the desk and waited for the procession to begin.

The name of the planet was MacTavish IV (if you went by the official Terran listing) or Ghryne (if you called it by what its people were accustomed to calling it). I thought of it privately as MacTavish IV and referred to it publicly as Ghryne. I believe in keeping the locals happy wherever I go.

Through the front window of the office, I could see our big gay tridim sign plastered to a facing wall: WANTED —EXTRATERRESTRIALS! We had saturated MacTavish IV with our promotional poop for a month preceding arrival. Stuff like this:

Want to visit Earth—see the Galaxy's most glittering and exclusive world? Want to draw good pay, work short hours, experience the thrills of show business on romantic Terra? If you are a nonterrestrial, there may be a place for you in the Corrigan Institute of Morphological Science. No freaks wanted—normal beings only. J. F. Corrigan will hold interviews in person on Ghryne from Thirdday to Fifthday of Tenmonth. His last visit to the Caledonia Cluster until 2937, so don't miss your chance! Hurry! A life of wonder and riches can be yours!

Broadsides like that, distributed wholesale in half a thousand languages, always bring them running. And the Corrigan Institute really packs in the crowds back on Earth. Why not? It's the best of its kind, the only really decent place where Earthmen can get a gander at the other species of the universe.

The office buzzer sounded. Auchinleck said unctuously, "The first applicant is ready to see you, sir."

"Send him, her or it in."

The door opened and a timid-looking life form advanced toward me on nervous little legs. He was a globular creature about the size of a big basketball, yellowish green, with two spindly double-kneed legs and five double-elbowed arms, the latter spaced regularly around his body. There was a lidless eye at the top of his head and five lidded ones, one above each arm. Plus a big, gaping toothless mouth.

His voice was a surprising resounding basso. "You are Mr. Corrigan?"

"That's right." I reached for a data blank. "Before we begin, I'll need certain information about—"

"I am a being of Regulus II," came the grave, booming reply, even before I had picked up the blank. "I need no special care and I am not a fugitive from the law of any world."

"Your name?"

"Lawrence R. Fitzgerald."

I throttled my exclamation of surprise, concealing it behind a quick cough. "Let me have that again, please?"

"Certainly. My name is Lawrence R. Fitzgerald. The 'R' stands for Raymond."

"Of course, that's not the name you were born with."

The being closed his eyes and toddled around in a 360-degree rotation, remaining in place. On his world, that gesture is the equivalent of an apologetic smile. "My Regullan name no longer matters. I am now and shall evermore be Lawrence R. Fitzgerald. I am a Terraphile, you see."

The little Regulan was as good as hired. Only the formalities remained. "You understand our terms, Mr. Fitzgerald?"

"I'll be placed on exhibition at your institute on Earth. You'll pay for my services, transportation and expenses. I'll be required to remain on exhibit no more than one-third of each Terran sidereal day."

"And the pay will be—ah—$50 Galactic a week, plus expenses and transportation."

The spherical creature clapped his hands in joy, three hands clapping on one side, two on the other. "Wonderful! I will see Earth at last! I accept the terms!"

I buzzed for Ludlow and gave him the fast signal that meant we were signing this alien up at half the usual pay, and Ludlow took him into the other office to sign him up.

I grinned, pleased with myself. We needed a green Regulan in our show; the last one had quit four years ago. But just because we needed him didn't mean we had to be extravagant in hiring him. A Terraphile alien who goes to the extent of rechristening himself with a Terran monicker would work for nothing, or even pay us, just so long as we let him get to Earth. My conscience won't let me really

40

exploit a being, but I don't believe in throwing money away, either.

The next applicant was a beefy ursinoid from Aldebaran IX. Our outfit has all the ursinoids it needs or is likely to need in the next few decades, and so I got rid of him in a couple of minutes. He was followed by a roly-poly blue-skinned humanoid from Donovan's Planet, four feet high and five hundred pounds heavy. We already had a couple of his species in the show, but they made good crowd-pleasers, being so plump and cheerful. I passed him along to Auchinleck to sign at anything short of top rate.

Next came a bedraggled Sirian spider who was more interested in a handout than a job. If there's any species we have a real oversupply of, it's those silver-colored spiders, but this seedy specimen gave it a try anyway. He got the gate in half a minute, and he didn't even get the handout he was angling for. I don't approve of begging.

The flow of applicants was steady. Ghryne is in the heart of the Caledonia Cluster, where the interstellar crossroads meet. We had figured to pick up plenty of new exhibits here and we were right.

It was the isolationism of the late 29th century that turned me into the successful proprietor of Corrigan's Institute, after some years as an impoverished carnival man in the Betelgeuse system. Back in 2903, the World Congress declared Terra off bounds for nonterrestrial beings, as an offshoot of the Terra for Terrans movement.

Before then, anyone could visit Earth. After the gate clanged down, a nonterrestrial could only get onto Sol III as a specimen in a scientific collection—in short, as an exhibit in a zoo.

That's what the Corrigan Institute of Morphological Science really is, of course. A zoo. But we don't go out and hunt for our specimens; we advertise and they come

41

flocking to us. Every alien wants to see Earth once in his lifetime, and there's only one way he can do it.

We don't keep too big an inventory. At last count, we had 690 specimens before this trip, representing 298 different intelligent life forms. My goal is at least one member of at least 500 different races. When I reach that, I'll sit back and let the competition catch up—if it can.

After an hour of steady work that morning, we had signed eleven new specimens. At the same time, we had turned away a dozen ursinoids, fifty of the reptilian natives of Ghryne, seven Sirian spiders, and no less than nineteen chlorine-breathing Procyonites wearing gas masks.

It was also my sad duty to nix a Vegan who was negotiating through a Ghrynian agent. A Vegan would be a top-flight attraction, being some 400 feet long and appropriately fearsome to the eye, but I didn't see how we could take one on. They're gentle and likable beings, but their upkeep runs into literally tons of fresh meat a day, and not just any old kind of meat either. So we had to do without the Vegan.

"One more specimen before lunch," I told Stebbins, "to make it an even dozen."

He looked at me queerly and nodded. A being entered. I took a long close look at the life form when it came in, and after that I took another one. I wondered what kind of stunt was being pulled. So far as I could tell, the being was quite plainly nothing but an Earthman.

He sat down facing me without being asked and crossed his legs. He was tall and extremely thin, with pale blue eyes and dirty blond hair, and though he was clean and reasonably well dressed, he had a shabby look about him. He said, in level Terran accents, "I'm looking for a job with your outfit, Corrigan."

"There's been a mistake. We're interested in nonterrestrials only."

"I'm a nonterrestrial. My name is Ildwar Gorb, of the planet Wazzenazz XIII."

I don't mind conning the public from time to time, but I draw the line at getting bilked myself. "Look, friend, I'm busy, and I'm not known for my sense of humor. Or my generosity."

"I'm not panhandling. I'm looking for a job."

"Then try elsewhere. Suppose you stop wasting my time, bud. You're as Earthborn as I am."

"I've never been within a dozen parsecs of Earth," he said smoothly. "I happen to be a representative of the only Earthlike race that exists anywhere in the Galaxy but on Earth itself. Wazzenazz XIII is a small and little-known planet in the Crab Nebula. Through an evolutionary fluke, my race is identical with yours. Now, don't you want me in your circus?"

"No. And it's not a circus. It's—"

"A scientific institute. I stand corrected."

There was something glib and appealing about this preposterous phony. I guess I recognized a kindred spirit or I would have tossed him out on his ear without another word. Instead I played along. "If you're from such a distant place, how come you speak English so well?"

"I'm not speaking. I'm a telepath—not the kind that reads minds, just the kind that projects. I communicate in symbols that you translate back to colloquial speech."

"Very clever, Mr. Gorb." I grinned at him and shook my head. "You spin a good yarn—but for my money, you're really Sam Jones or Phil Smith from Earth, stranded here and out of cash. You want a free trip back to Earth. No deal. The demand for beings from Wazzenazz XIII is pretty low these days. Zero, in fact. Good-bye, Mr. Gorb."

He pointed a finger squarely at me and said, "You're making a big mistake. I'm just what your outfit needs. A representative of a hitherto utterly unknown race identical to humanity in every respect! Look here, examine my teeth. Absolutely like human teeth! And—"

I pulled away from his yawning mouth. "Good-bye, Mr. Gorb," I repeated.

"All I ask is a contract, Corrigan. It isn't much. I'll be a big attraction. I'll—"

"Good-bye, Mr. Gorb!"

He glowered at me reproachfully for a moment, stood up and sauntered to the door. "I thought you were a man of acumen, Corrigan. Well, think it over. Maybe you'll regret your hastiness. I'll be back to give you another chance."

He slammed the door and I let my grim expression relax into a smile. This was the best con switch yet—an Earthman posing as an alien to get a job!

But I wasn't buying it, even if I could appreciate his cleverness intellectually. There's no such place as Wazzenazz XIII and there's only one human race in the Galaxy —on Earth. I was going to need some real good reason before I gave a down-and-out grifter a free ticket home.

I didn't know it then, but before the day was out, I would have that reason. And, with it, plenty of trouble on my hands.

The first harbinger of woe turned up after lunch in the person of a Kallerian. The Kallerian was the sixth applicant that afternoon. I had turned away three more ursinoids, hired a vegetable from Miazan, and said no to a scaly pseudo-armadillo from one of the Delta Worlds. Hardly had the 'dillo scuttled dejectedly out of my office when the Kallerian came striding in, not even waiting for Stebbins to admit him officially.

He was big even for his kind—in the neighborhood of nine feet high, and getting on toward a ton. He planted himself firmly on his three stocky feet, extended his massive arms in a Kallerian greeting gesture, and growled, "I am

44

Vallo Heraal, Freeman of Kaller IV. You will sign me immediately to a contract."

"Sit down, Freeman Heraal. I like to make my own decisions, thanks."

"You will grant me a contract!"

"Will you please sit down?"

He said sulkily, "I will remain standing."

"As you prefer." My desk has a few concealed features which are sometimes useful in dealing with belligerent or disappointed life forms. My fingers roamed to the meshgun trigger, just in case of trouble.

The Kallerian stood motionless before me. They're hairy creatures, and this one had a coarse, thick mat of blue fur completely covering his body. Two fierce eyes glimmered out through the otherwise dense blanket of fur. He was wearing the kilt, girdle and ceremonial blaster of his warlike race.

I said, "You'll have to understand, Freeman Heraal, that it's not our policy to maintain more than a few members of each species at our Institute. And we're not currently in need of any Kallerian males, because—"

"You will hire me or trouble I will make!"

I opened our inventory chart. I showed him that we were already carrying four Kallerians, and that was more than plenty.

The beady little eyes flashed like beacons in the fur. "Yes, you have four representatives—of the Clan Verdrokh! None of the Clan Gursdrinn! For three years, I have waited for a chance to avenge this insult to the noble Clan Gursdrinn!"

At the key word *avenge*, I readied myself to ensnarl the Kallerian in a spume of tanglemesh the instant he went for his blaster, but he didn't move. He bellowed, "I have vowed a vow, Earthman. Take me to Earth, enroll a Gursdrinn, or the consequences will be terrible!"

I'm a man of principles, like all straightforward double-

45

dealers, and one of the most important of those principles is that I never let myself be bullied by anyone. "I deeply regret having unintentionally insulted your clan, Freeman Heraal. Will you accept my apologies?"

He glared at me in silence.

I went on, "Please be assured that I'll undo the insult at the earliest possible opportunity. It's not feasible for us to hire another Kallerian now, but I'll give preference to the Clan Gursdrinn as soon as a vacancy—"

"No. You will hire me now."

"It can't be done, Freeman Heraal. We have a budget, and we stick to it."

"You will rue! I will take drastic measures!"

"Threats will get you nowhere, Freeman Heraal. I give you my word I'll get in touch with you as soon as our organization has room for another Kallerian. And now, please, there are many applicants waiting—"

You'd think it would be sort of humiliating to become a specimen in a zoo, but most of these races take it as an honor. And there's always the chance that, by picking a given member of a race, we're insulting all the others.

I nudged the trouble button on the side of my desk and Auchinleck and Ludlow appeared simultaneously from the two doors at right and left. They surrounded the towering Kallerian and sweet-talking led him away. He wasn't minded to quarrel physically, or he could have knocked them both into the next city with a backhand swipe of his shaggy paw, but he kept up a growling flow of invective and threats until he was out in the hall.

I mopped sweat from my forehead and began to buzz Stebbins for the next applicant. But before my finger touched the button, the door popped open and a small being came scooting in, followed by an angry Stebbins.

"Come here, you!"

"Stebbins?" I said gently.

46

"I'm sorry, Mr. Corrigan. I lost sight of this one for a moment, and he came running in—"

"Please, please," squeaked the little alien pitifully. "I must see you, honored sir!"

"It isn't his turn in line," Stebbins protested. "There are at least fifty ahead of him."

"All right," I said tiredly. "As long as he's in here already, I might as well see him. Be more careful next time, Stebbins."

Stebbins nodded dolefully and backed out.

The alien was a pathetic sight: a Stortulian, a squirrely-looking creature about three feet high. His fur, which should have been a lustrous black, was a dull gray, and his eyes were wet and sad. His tail drooped. His voice was little more than a faint whimper, even at full volume.

"Begging your most honored pardon most humbly, important sir. I am a being of Stortul XII, having sold my last few possessions to travel to Ghryne for the miserable purpose of obtaining an interview with yourself."

I said, "I'd better tell you right at the outset that we're already carrying our full complement of Stortulians. We have both a male and a female now and—"

"This is known to me. The female—is her name perchance Tiress?"

I glanced down at the inventory chart until I found the Stortulian entry. "Yes, that's her name."

The little being immediately emitted a soul-shaking gasp. "It is she! It is she!"

"I'm afraid we don't have room for any more—"

"You are not in full understanding of my plight. The female Tiress, she is—was—my own Fire-sent spouse, my comfort and my warmth, my life and my love."

"Funny," I said. "When we signed her three years ago, she said she was single. It's right here on the chart."

"She lied! She left my burrow because she longed to see

47

the splendours of Earth. And I am alone, bound by our sacred customs never to remarry, languishing in sadness and pining for her return. You *must* take me to Earth! "

"But—"

"I must see her—her and this disgrace-bringing lover of hers. I must reason with her. Earthman, can't you see I must appeal to her inner flame? *I must bring her back!*"

My face was expressionless. "You don't really intend to join our organization at all—you just want free passage to Earth?"

"Yes, yes!" wailed the Stortulian. "Find some other member of my race, if you must! Let me have my wife again, Earthman! Is your heart a dead lump of stone?"

It isn't, but another of my principles is to refuse to be swayed by sentiment. I felt sorry for this being's domestic troubles, but I wasn't going to break up a good act just to make an alien squirrel happy—not to mention footing the transportation.

I said, "I don't see how we can manage it. The laws are very strict on the subject of bringing alien life to Earth. It has to be for scientific purposes only. And if I know in advance that your purpose in coming isn't scientific, I can't in all conscience lie for you, can I?"

"Well—"

"Of course not." I took advantage of his pathetic upset to steam right along. "Now if you had come in here and simply asked me to sign you up, I might conceivably have done it. But no—you had to go unburden your heart to me."

"I thought the truth would move you."

"It did. But in effect you're now asking me to conspire in a fraudulent criminal act. Friend, I can't do it. My reputation means too much to me," I said piously.

"Then you will refuse me?"

"My heart melts to nothingness for you. But I can't take you to Earth."

48

"Perhaps you will send my wife to me here?"

There's a clause in every contract that allows me to jettison an unwanted specimen. All I have to do is declare it no longer of scientific interest, and the World Government will deport the undesirable alien back to its home world. But I wouldn't pull a low trick like that on our female Stortulian.

I said, "I'll ask her about coming home. But I won't ship her back against her will. And maybe she's happier where she is."

The Stortulian seemed to shrivel. His eyelids closed halfway to mask his tears. He turned and shambled slowly to the door, walking like a living dishrag. In a bleak voice, he said, "There is no hope then. All is lost. I will never see my soulmate again. Good day, Earthman."

He spoke in a drab monotone that almost, but not quite, had me weeping. I watched him shuffle out. I do have some conscience, and I had the uneasy feeling I had just been talking to a being who was about to commit suicide on my account.

About fifty more applicants were processed without a hitch. Then life started to get complicated again.

Nine of the fifty were okay. The rest were unacceptable for one reason or another, and they took the bad news quietly enough. The haul for the day so far was close to two dozen new life forms under contract.

I had just about begun to forget about the incidents of the Kallerian's outraged pride and the Stortulian's flighty wife when the door opened and the Earthman who called himself Ildwar Gorb of Wazzenazz XIII stepped in.

"How did *you* get in here?" I demanded.

"Your man happened to be looking the wrong way," he said cheerily. "Change your mind about me yet?"

"Get out before I have you thrown out."

Gorb shrugged. "I figured you hadn't changed your mind, so I've changed my pitch a bit. If you won't believe

I'm from Wazzenazz XIII, suppose I tell you that I *am* Earthborn, and that I'm looking for a job on your staff."

"I don't care *what* your story is! Get out or—"

"—you'll have me thrown out. Okay, okay. Just give me half a second. Corrigan, you're no fool, and neither am I —but that fellow of yours outside is. He doesn't know how to handle alien beings. How many times today has a life form come in here unexpectedly?"

I scowled at him. "Too damn many."

"You see? He's incompetent. Suppose you fire him, take me on instead. I've been living in the outworlds half my life; I know all there is to know about alien life forms. You can use me, Corrigan."

I took a deep breath and glanced all around the paneled ceiling of the office before I spoke. "Listen, Gorb, or whatever your name is, I've had a hard day. There's been a Kallerian in here who just about threatened murder, and there's been a Stortulian in here who's about to commit suicide because of me. I have a conscience and it's troubling me. But get this: I just want to finish off my recruiting, pack up and go home to Earth. I don't want you hanging around here bothering me. I'm not looking to hire new staff members, and if you switch back to claiming you're an unknown life form from Wazzenazz XIII, the answer is that I'm not looking for any of those either. Now will you scram or—"

The office door crashed open at that point and Heraal, the Kallerian, came thundering in. He was dressed from head to toe in glittering metalfoil, and instead of his ceremonial blaster he was wielding a sword the length of a human being. Stebbins and Auchinleck came dragging helplessly along in his wake, hanging desperately to his belt.

"Sorry, chief," Stebbins gasped. "I tried to keep him out, but—"

Heraal, who had planted himself in front of my desk,

drowned him out with a roar. "Earthman, you have mortally insulted the Clan Gursdrinn!"

Sitting with my hands poised near the meshgun trigger, I was ready to let him have it at the first sight of actual violence.

Heraal boomed, "You are responsible for what is to happen now. I have notified the authorities and you prosecuted will be for causing the death of a life form! Suffer, Earthborn ape! Suffer!"

"Watch it, chief," Stebbins yelled. "He's going to—"

An instant before my numb fingers could tighten on the meshgun trigger, Heraal swung that huge sword through the air and plunged it savagely through his body. He toppled forward onto the carpet with the sword projecting a couple of feet out of his back. A few driblets of bluish-purple blood spread from beneath him.

Before I could react to the big life form's hari-kiri, the office door flew open again and three sleek reptilian beings entered, garbed in the green sashes of the local police force. Their golden eyes goggled down at the figure on the floor, then came to rest on me.

"You are J. F. Corrigan?" the leader asked.

"Y-yes."

"We have received word of complaint against you. Said complaint being—"

"—that your unethical actions have directly contributed to the untimely death of an intelligent life form," filled in the second of the Ghrynian policemen.

"The evidence lies before us," intoned the leader, "in the cadaver of the unfortunate Kallerian who filed the complaint with us several minutes ago."

"And therefore," said the third lizard, "it is our duty to arrest you for this crime and declare you subject to a fine of no less than $100,000 Galactic or two years in prison."

"Hold on!" I stormed. "You mean that any being from

51

anywhere in the Universe can come in here and gut himself on my carpet, and *I'm* responsible?"

"This is the law. D'you deny that your stubborn refusal to yield to this late life form's request lies at the root of his sad demise?"

"Well, no, but—"

"Failure to deny is admission of guilt. You are guilty, Earthman."

Closing my eyes wearily, I tried to wish the whole babbling lot of them away. If I had to, I could pony up the hundred-grand fine, but it was going to put an awful dent in this year's take. And I shuddered when I remembered that any minute that scrawny little Stortulian was likely to come bursting in here to kill himself too. Was it a fine of $100,000 per suicide? At that rate, I could be out of business by nightfall.

I was spared further such morbid thoughts by yet another unannounced arrival.

The small figure of the Stortulian trudged through the open doorway and stationed itself limply near the threshold. The three Ghrynian policemen and my three assistants forgot the dead Kallerian for a moment and turned to eye the newcomer.

I had visions of unending troubles with the law here on Ghryne. I resolved never to come here on a recruiting trip again—or, if I *did* come, to figure out some more effective way of screening myself against crackpots.

In heartrending tones, the Stortulian declared, "Life is no longer worth living. My last hope is gone. There is only one thing left for me to do."

I was quivering at the thought of another hundred thousand smackers going down the drain. "Stop him, somebody! He's going to kill himself! He's—"

Then somebody sprinted toward me, hit me amidships, and knocked me flying out from behind my desk before I had a chance to fire the meshgun. My head walloped the floor, and for five or six seconds, I guess I wasn't fully aware of what was going on.

Gradually the scene took shape around me. There was a monstrous hole in the wall behind my desk; a smoking blaster lay on the floor, and I saw the three Ghrynian policemen sitting on the raving Stortulian. The man who called himself Ildwar Gorb was getting to his feet and dusting himself off.

He helped me up. "Sorry to have had to tackle you, Corrigan. But that Stortulian wasn't here to commit suicide, you see. He was out to get you."

I weaved dizzily toward my desk and dropped into my chair. A flying fragment of wall had deflated my pneumatic cushion. The smell of ashed plaster was everywhere. The police were effectively cocooning the struggling little alien in an unbreakable tanglemesh.

"Evidently you don't know as much as you think you do about Stortulian psychology, Corrigan," Gorb said lightly. "Suicide is completely abhorrent to them. When they're troubled, they kill the person who caused their trouble. In this case, you."

I began to chuckle—more of a tension-relieving snicker than a full-bodied laugh.

"Funny," I said.

"What is?" asked the self-styled Wazzenazzian.

"These aliens. Big blustery Heraal came in with murder in his eye and killed *himself*, and the pint-sized Stortulian who looked so meek and pathetic damn near blew my head off." I shuddered. "Thanks for the tackle job."

"Don't mention it," Gorb said.

I glared at the Ghrynian police. "Well? What are you waiting for? Take that murderous little beast out of here! Or isn't murder against the local laws?"

"The Stortulian will be duly punished," replied the leaders of the Ghrynian cops calmly. "But there is the matter of the dead Kallerian and the fine of—"

53

"—one hundred thousand dollars. I know." I groaned and turned to Stebbins. "Get the Terran Consulate on the phone, Stebbins. Have them send down a legal adviser. Find out if there's any way we can get out of this mess with our skins intact."

"Right, chief." Stebbins moved toward the visiphone.

Gorb stepped forward and put a hand on his chest.

"Hold it," the Wazzenazzian said crisply. "The Consulate can't help you. I can."

"You?" I said.

"I can get you out of this cheap."

"*How* cheap?"

Gorb grinned rakishly. "Five thousand in cash plus a contract as a specimen with your outfit. In advance, of course. That's a heck of a lot better than forking over a hundred grand, isn't it?"

I eyed Gorb uncertainly. The Terran Consulate people probably wouldn't be much help; they tried to keep out of local squabbles unless they were really serious, and I knew from past experiences that no officials ever worried much about the state of my pocketbook. On the other hand, giving this slyster a contract might be a risky proposition.

"Tell you what," I said finally. "You've got yourself a deal—but on a contingency basis. Get me out of this and you'll have five grand and the contract. Otherwise, nothing."

Gorb shrugged. "What have I to lose?"

Before the police could interfere, Gorb trotted over to the hulking corpse of the Kallerian and fetched it a mighty kick.

"Wake up, you faker! Stop playing possum and stand up! You aren't fooling anyone!"

The Ghrynians got off the huddled little assassin and tried to stop Gorb. "Your pardon, but the dead require your respect," began one of the lizards mildly.

Gorb whirled angrily. "Maybe the dead do—but this character isn't dead!"

He knelt and said loudly in the Kallerian's dishlike ear, "You might as well quit it, Heraal. Listen to this, you shamming mountain of meat—*your mother knits doilies for the Clan Verdrokh!*"

The supposedly dead Kallerian emitted a twenty-cycle rumble that shook the floor, and clambered to his feet, pulling the sword out of his body and waving it in the air. Gorb leaped back nimbly, snatched up the Stortulian's fallen blaster, and trained it neatly on the big alien's throat before he could do any damage. The Kallerian grumbled and lowered his sword.

I felt groggy. I thought I knew plenty about nonterrestrial lifeforms, but I was learning a few things today. "I don't understand. How—"

The police were blue with chagrin. "A thousand pardons, Earthman. There seems to have been some error."

"There seems to have been a cute little con game," Gorb remarked quietly.

I recovered my balance. "Try to milk me of a hundred grand when there's been no crime?" I snapped. "I'll say there's been an error! If I weren't a forgiving man, I'd clap the bunch of you in jail for attempting to defraud an Earthman! Get out of here! And take that would-be murderer with you!"

They got, and they got fast, burbling apologies as they went. They had tried to fox an Earthman, and that's a dangerous sport. They dragged the cocooned form of the Stortulian with them. The air seemed to clear, and peace was restored. I signaled to Auchinleck and he slammed the door.

"All right." I looked at Gorb and jerked a thumb at the Kallerian. "That's a nice trick. How does it work?"

Gorb smiled pleasantly. He was enjoying this, I could see. "Kallerians of the Clan Gursdrinn specialize in a kind of mental discipline, Corrigan. It isn't too widely known in this area of the Galaxy, but men of that clan have unusual mental control over their bodies. They can cut off circulation and nervous-system response in large chunks of their bodies for hours at a stretch—an absolutely perfect imitation of death. And, of course, when Heraal put the sword through himself, it was a simple matter to avoid hitting any vital organ en route."

The Kallerian, still at gunpoint, hung his head in shame. I turned on him. "So—try to swindle me, eh? You cooked up this whole fake suicide in collusion with those cops."

He looked quite a sight, with that gaping slash running clear through his body. But the wound had begun to heal already. "I regret the incident, Earthman. I am mortified. Be good enough to destroy this unworthy person."

It was a tempting idea, but a notion was forming in my showman's mind. "No, I won't destroy you. Tell me—how often can you do that trick?"

"The tissues will regenerate in a few hours."

"Would you mind having to kill yourself every day, Heraal? And twice on Sundays?"

Heraal looked doubtful. "Well, for the honor of my clan, perhaps—"

Stebbins said, "Boss, you mean—"

"Shut up. Heraal, you're hired—$75 a week plus expenses. Stebbins, get me a contract form—and type in a clause requring Heraal to perform his suicide stunt at least five but no more than eight times a week."

I felt a satisfied glow. There's nothing more pleasing than to turn a swindle into a sure-fire crowd puller.

"Aren't you forgetting something, Corrigan?" asked Ildwar Gorb in a quietly menacing voice. "We had a little agreement, you know."

"Oh. Yes." I moistened my lips and glanced shiftily around the office. There had been too many witnesses. I couldn't back down. I had no choice but to write out a check for five grand and give Gorb a standard alien-specimen contract. Unless. . . .

"Just a second," I said. "To enter Earth as an alien exhibit, you need proof of alien origin."

He grinned, pulled out a batch of documents. "Nothing to it. Everything's stamped and in order—and anybody who wants to prove these papers are fraudulent will have to find Wazzenazz XIII first!"

We signed and I filed the contracts away. But only then did it occur to me that the events of the past hour might have been even more complicated than they looked. Suppose, I wondered, Gorb had conspired with Heraal to stage the fake suicide, and rung in the cops as well—with contracts for both of them the price of my getting off the hook?

It could very well be. And if it was, it meant I had been taken as neatly as any chump I'd ever conned.

Carefully keeping a poker face, I did a silent burn. Gorb, or whatever his real name was, was going to find himself living up to that contract he'd signed—every damn word and letter of it!

We left Ghryne later that week, having interviewed some eleven hundred alien forms and having hired fifty-two. It brought the register of our zoo—pardon me, the institute— to a nice pleasant 742 specimens representing 326 intelligent life forms.

Ildwar Gorb, the Wazzenazzian—who admitted that his real name was Mike Higgins, of St. Louis—turned out to be a tower of strength on the return voyage. It developed that he really *did* know all there was to know about alien life forms.

When he found out I had turned down the 400-foot-long Vegan because the upkeep would be too big, Gorb-Higgins rushed off to the Vegan's agent and concluded a deal whereby we acquired a fertilized Vegan ovum, weighing hardly more than an ounce. Transporting *that* was a

57

lot cheaper than lugging a full-grown adult Vegan. Besides which, he assured me that the infant beast could be adapted to a diet of vegetables without any difficulty.

He made life a lot easier for me during the six-week voyage to Earth in our specially constructed ship. With fifty-two alien life forms aboard, all sorts of dietary problems arose, not to mention the headaches that popped up over pride of place and the like. The Kallerian simply refused to be quartered anywhere but on the left-hand side of the ship, for example—but that was the side we had reserved for low-gravity creatures, and there was no room for him there.

"We'll be traveling in hyperspace all the way to Earth," Gorb-Higgins assured the stubborn Kallerian. "Our cosmostatic polarity will be reversed, you see."

"Hah?" asked Heraal in confusion.

"The cosmostatic polarity. If you take a bunk on the left-hand side of the ship, you'll be traveling on the right-hand side all the way there!"

"Oh," said the big Kallerian. "I didn't know that. Thank you for explaining."

He gratefully took the stateroom we assigned him.

Higgins really had a way with the creatures, all right. He made us look like fumbling amateurs, and I had been operating in this business more than fifteen years.

Somehow Higgins managed to be on the spot whenever trouble broke out. A high-strung Norvennith started a feud with a pair of Vanoinans over an alleged moral impropriety; Norvennithi can be *very* stuffy sometimes. But Gorb convinced the outraged being that what the Vanoinans were doing in the washroom was perfectly proper. Well, it was, but I'd never have thought of using that particular analogy.

I could list half a dozen other incidents in which Gorb-Higgins' special knowledge of outworld beings saved us from annoying hassles on that trip back. It was the first time I had ever had another man with brains in the organization and I was getting worried.

When I first set up the institute back in the early 2920s, it was with my own capital, scraped together while running a comparative biology show on Betelgeuse IX. I saw to it that I was the sole owner. And I took care to hire competent but unspectacular men as my staffers—men like Stebbins, Auchinleck and Ludlow.

Only now I had a viper in my bosom, in the person of this Ildwar Gorb-Mike Higgins. He could think for himself. He knew a good racket when he saw one. We were birds of a feather, Higgins and I. I doubted if there was room for both of us in this outfit.

I sent for him just before we were about to make Earthfall, offered him a few slugs of brandy before I got to the point. "Mike, I've watched the way you handled the exhibits on the way back here."

"The *other* exhibits," he pointed out. "I'm one of them, not a staff man."

"Your Wazzenazzian status is just a fiction cooked up to get you past the immigration authorities, Mike. But I've got a proposition for you."

"Propose away."

"I'm getting a little too old for this starcombing routine," I said. "Up to now, I've been doing my own recruiting, but only because I couldn't trust anyone else to do the job. I think you could handle it, though." I stubbed out my cigarette and lit another. "Tell you what, Mike—I'll rip up your contract as an exhibit, and I'll give you another one as a staffman, paying twice as much. Your job will be to roam the planets finding new material for us. How about it?"

I had the new contract all drawn up. I pushed it toward him, but he put his hand down over mine and smiled amiably as he said, "No go."

"No? Not even for twice the pay?"

59

"I've done my own share of roaming," he said. "Don't offer me more money. I just want to settle down on Earth, Jim. I don't care about the cash. Honest."

It was very touching, and also very phony, but there was nothing I could do. I couldn't get rid of him that way. I had to bring him to Earth.

The immigration officials argued about his papers, but he'd had the things so cleverly faked that there was no way of proving he wasn't from Wazzenazz XIII. We set him up in a key spot of the building.

The Kallerian, Heraal, is one of our top attractions now. Every day at two in the afternoon, he commits ritual suicide, and soon afterwards rises from death to the accompaniment of a trumpet fanfare. The four other Kallerians we had before are wildly jealous of the crowds he draws, but they're just not trained to do his act.

But the unquestioned number-one attraction here is confidence man Mike Higgins, He's billed as the only absolutely human life form from an extraterrestrial planet, and though we've had our share of debunking, it has only increased business.

Funny that the biggest draw at a zoo like ours should be a homegrown Earthman, but that's show business.

A couple of weeks after we got back, Mike added a new wrinkle to the act. He turned up with a blonde showgirl named Marie, and now we have a woman from Wazzenazz too. It's more fun for Mike that way. And downright clever.

He's too clever, in fact. Like I said, I appreciate a good confidence man, the way some people appreciate fine wine. But I wish I had left Ildwar Gorb back on Ghryne, instead of signing him up with us.

Yesterday he stopped by at my office after we had closed down for the day. He was wearing that pleasant smile he always wears when he's up to something.

60

He accepted a drink, as usual, and then he said, "Jim, I was talking to Lawrence R. Fitzgerald yesterday."

"The little Regulan? The green basketball?"

"That's the one. He tells me he's only getting $50 a week. And a lot of the other boys here are drawing pretty low pay too."

My stomach gave a warning twinge. "Mike, if you're looking for a raise, I've told you time and again you're worth it to me. How about twenty a week?"

He held up one hand. "I'm not angling for a raise for *me*, Jim."

"What then?"

He smiled beatifically. "The boys and I held a little meeting yesterday evening, and we—ah—formed a union, with me as leader. I'd like to discuss the idea of a general wage increase for every one of the exhibits here."

"Higgins, you blackmailer, how can I afford—"

"Easy," he said. "You'd hate to lose a few weeks' gross, wouldn't you?"

"You mean you'd call a strike?"

He shrugged. "If you leave me no choice, how else can I protect my members' interests?"

After about half an hour of haggling, he sweated me into an across-the-board increase for the entire mob, with a distinct hint of further raises to come. But he also casually let me know the price he's asking to call off the hounds. He wants a partnership in the institute; a share in the receipts.

If he gets that, it makes him a member of management, and he'll have to quit as union leader. That way I won't have him to contend with as a negotiator.

But I *will* have him firmly embedded in the organization, and once he gets his foot in the door, he won't be satisfied until he's on top—which means when I'm out.

But I'm not licked yet! Not after a full lifetime of conniving and swindling! I've been over and over the angles and there's one thing you can always count on—a trickster will always outsmart himself if you give him the chance. I did it with Higgins. Now he's done it with me.

He'll be back here in half an hour to find out whether he gets his partnership or not. Well, he'll get his answer. I'm going to affirm, as per the escape clause in the standard exhibit contract he signed, that he is no longer of scientific value, and the Feds will pick him up and deport him to his home world.

That leaves him two equally nasty choices.

Those fake documents of his were good enough to get him admitted to Earth as a legitimate alien. How the World Police get him back there is their headache—and his.

If he admits the papers were phony, the only way he'll get out of prison will be when it collapses of old age.

So I'll give him a third choice: He can sign an undated confession, which I will keep in my safe, as guarantee against future finagling.

I don't expect to be around forever, you see, though, with that little secret I picked up on Rimbaud II, it'll be a good long time, not even barring accidents, and I've been wondering whom to leave the Corrigan Institute of Morphological Science to. Higgins will make a fine successor.

Oh, one more thing he will have to sign. It remains the Corrigan Institute as long as the place is in business.

Try to outcon me, will he?

THERE WAS AN OLD WOMAN—

Since I was raised from earliest infancy to undertake the historian's calling, and since it is now certain that I shall never claim that profession as my own, it seems fitting that I perform my first and last act as an historian.

I shall write the history of that strange and unique woman, the mother of my thirty brothers and myself, Miss Donna Mitchell.

She was a person of extraordinary strength and vision, our mother. I remember her vividly, seeing her with all her sons gathered round her in our secluded Wisconsin farmhouse on the first night of summer, after we had returned to her from every part of the country for our summer's vacation. One-and-thirty strapping sons, each one of us six feet one inch tall, with a shock of unruly yellow hair and keen, clear blue eyes, each one of us healthy, strong, well-nourished, each one of us twenty-one years and fourteen days old—one-and-thirty identical brothers.

Oh, there were differences between us, but only we and she could perceive them. To outsiders, we were identical; which was why, to outsiders, we took care never to appear together in groups. We ourselves knew the differences, for we had lived with them for so long.

I knew my brother Leonard's cheekmole—the right cheek it was, setting him off from Jonas, whose left cheek was marked with a flyspeck. I knew the faint tilt of Peter's chin, the slight oversharpness of Dewey's nose, the florid tint of Donald's skin. I recognized Paul by his pendulous earlobes, Charles by his squint, Noel by the puckering of his lower lip. David had a blue-stubbled face, Mark flaring nostrils, Claude thick brows.

Yes, there were differences. We rarely confused one with another. It was second nature for me to distinguish Edward from Albert, George from Philip, Frederick from Stephen. And Mother *never* confused us.

She was a regal woman, nearly six feet in height, who even in middle age had retained straightness of posture and majesty of bearing. Her eyes, like ours, were blue; her hair, she told us, had once been golden like ours. Her voice was a deep, mellow contralto; rich, firm, commanding, the voice of a strong woman. She had been professor of Biochemistry at some Eastern university (she never told us which one, hating its name so) and we all knew by heart the story of her bitter life and of our own strange birth.

"I had a theory," she would say. "It wasn't an orthodox theory, and it made people angry to think about it, so of course they threw me out. But I didn't care. In many ways that was the most fortunate day of my life."

"Tell us about it, Mother," Philip would invariably ask. He was destined to be a playwright; he enjoyed the repetition of the story whenever we were together.

She said:

"I had a theory. I believed that environment controlled personality, that given the same set of healthy genes any number of different adults could be shaped from the raw material. I had a plan for testing it—but when I told them, they discharged me. Luckily I had married a wealthy if superficial-minded executive, who had suffered a fatal coronary attack the year before. I was independently wealthy, thanks to him, and free to pursue independent research, thanks to my university discharge. So I came to Wisconsin and began my great project."

We knew the rest of the story by heart, as a sort of litany.

We knew how she had bought a huge, rambling farm in the flat green country of central Wisconsin, a farm far from prying eyes. Then, how on a hot summer afternoon she had gone forth to the farm land nearby, and found a field hand, tall and brawny, and to his great surprise seduced him in the field where he worked.

And then the story of that single miraculous zygote, which our mother had extracted from her body and carefully nurtured in special nutrient tanks, irradiating it and freezing it and irritating it and dosing it with hormones until, exasperated, it subdivided into thirty-two, each one of which developed independently into a complete embryo.

Embryo grew into fetus, and fetus into child, in Mother's ingenious artificial wombs. One of the thirty-two died before birth of accidental narcosis; the remainder survived, thirty-one identical males sprung from the same egg, to become us.

With the formidable energy that typified her, Mother single-handed nursed thirty-one baby boys; we thrived, we grew. And then the most crucial stage of the experiment began. We were differentiated at the age of eighteen months, each given his own room, his own particular toys, his own special books later on. Each of us was slated for a different profession. It was the ultimate proof of her theory. Genetically identical, physically identical except for the minor changes time had worked on our individual bodies, we would nevertheless seek out different fields of employ.

She worked out the assignments at random, she said. Philip was to be a playwright, Noel a novelist, Donald a doctor. Astronomy was Allan's goal, Barry's biology, Albert's the stage. George was to be a concert pianist, Claude a composer, Leonard a member of the bar, Dewey a dentist. Mark was to be an athlete; David, a diplomat. Journalism waited for Jonas, poetry for Peter, painting for Paul. Edward would become an engineer, Saul a soldier, Charles a statesman; Stephen would go to sea. Martin was aimed for chemistry, Raymond for physics, James for high finance. Ronald would be a librarian, Robert a bookkeeper, John a priest, Douglas a teacher. Anthony was to be a literary critic, William a librarian, Frederick an airplane pilot. For Richard was reserved a life of crime; as for myself, Harold, I was to devote my energies to the study and writing of history.

This was my mother's plan. Let me tell of my own childhood and adolescence, to illustrate its workings.

My first recollections are of books. I had a room on the second floor of our big house. Martin's room was to my left, and in later years I would regret it, for the air was always heavy with the stink of his chemical experiments. To my right was Noel, whose precocious typewriter sometimes pounded all night as he worked on his endless first novel.

But those manifestations came later. I remember waking one morning to find that during the night a bookcase had been placed in my room, and in it a single book— Hendrik Willem van Loon's *Story of Mankind*. I was four, almost five, then; thanks to Mother's intensive training we were all capable readers by that age, and I puzzled over the big type, learning of the exploits of Charlemagne and Richard the Lionhearted and staring at the squiggly scratches that were van Loon's illustrations.

Other books followed, in years to come. H. G. Wells' *Outline of History*, which fascinated and repelled me at the same time. Toynbee, in the Somervell abridgement, and later, when I had entered adolescence, the complete and unabridged edition. Churchill, and his flowing periods and ringing prose. Sandburg's poetic and massive life of

Lincoln; Wedgwood on the Thirty Years' War; Will Durant, in six or seven blocklike volumes.

I read these books, and where I did not understand I read on anyway, knowing I would come back to that page in some year to come and bring new understanding to it. Mother helped, and guided, and chivvied. A sense of the panorama of man's vast achievement sprang up in me. To join the roll of mankind's chroniclers seemed the only possible end for my existence.

Each summer from my fourteenth to my seventeenth, I traveled—alone, of course, since Mother wanted to build self-reliance in us. I visited the great historical places of the United States: Washington, D.C., Mount Vernon, Williamsburg, Bull Run, Gettysburg. A sense of the past rose in me.

Those summers were my only opportunities for contact with strangers, since during the year and especially during the long snowbound winters we stayed on the farm, a tight family unit. We never went to public school; obviously, it was impossible to enroll us, en masse, without arousing the curiosity my mother wished to avoid.

Instead, she tutored us privately, giving us care and attention that no professional teacher could possibly have supplied. And we grew older, diverging toward our professions like branching limbs of a tree.

As a future historian, of course, I took it upon myself to observe the changes in my own society, which was bounded by the acreage of our farm. I made notes on the progress of my brothers, keeping my notebooks well hidden, and also on the changes time was working on Mother. She stood up surprisingly well, considering the astonishing burden she had taken upon herself. Formidable was the best word to use in describing her.

We grew into adolescence. By this time Martin had an imposing chemical laboratory in his room; Leonard harangued us all on legal fine points, and Anthony pored over Proust and Kafka, delivering startling critical interpretations. Our house was a beehive of industry constantly, and I don't remember being bored for more than three consecutive seconds, at any time. There were always distractions: Claude and George jostling for room on the piano bench while they played Claude's four-hand sonata, Mark hurling a baseball through a front window, Peter declaiming a sequence of shocking sonnets during our communal dinner.

We fought, of course, since we were healthy individualists with sound bodies. Mother encouraged it; Saturday afternoon was wrestling time, and we pitted our growing strengths against one another.

Mother was always the dominant figure, striding tall and erect around the farm, calling to us in her familiar boom, assigning us chores, meeting with us privately. Somehow she had the knack of making each of us think we were the favorite child, the one in whose future she was most deeply interested of all. It was false, of course; though once Jonas unkindly asserted that Barry must be her *real* favorite, because he, like her, was a biologist.

I doubted it. I had learned much about people through my constant reading, and I knew that Mother was something extraordinary—a fanatic, if you like, or merely a woman driven by an inner demon, but still and all a person of overwhelming intellectual drive and conviction, whose will to know the truth had led her to undertake this fantastic experiment in biology and human breeding.

I knew that no woman of that sort could stoop to petty favoritism. Mother was unique. Perhaps, had she been born a man, she would have changed the entire course of human development.

When we were seventeen, she called us all together round the big table in the common room of our rambling home. She waited, needing to clear her throat only once in order to cut the hum of conversation.

"Sons," she said, and the echo rang through the entire first floor of the house. "Sons, the time has come for you to leave the farm."

We were stunned, even those of us who were expecting it. But she explained, and we understood, and we did not quarrel.

One could not become a doctor or a chemist or a novelist or even an historian in a total vacuum. One had to enter the world. And one needed certain professional qualifications.

We were going to college.

Not all of us, of course. Robert was to be a bookkeeper; he would go to business school. Mark had developed, through years of practice, into a superb right-handed pitcher, and he was to go to Milwaukee for a major-league tryout. Claude and George, aspiring composer and aspiring pianist, would attend an Eastern conservatory together, posing as twins.

The rest of us were to attend colleges, and those who were to go on to professions such as medicine or chemistry would plan to attend professional schools afterward. Mother believed the college education was essential, even to a poet or a painter or a novelist.

Only one of us was not sent to any accredited institution. He was Richard, who was to be our criminal. Already he had made several sallies into the surrounding towns and cities, returning a few days or a few weeks later with money or jewels and with a guilty grin on his face. He was simply to be turned loose into the school of Life, and Mother warned him never to get caught.

As for me, I was sent to Princeton and enrolled as a liberal-arts student. Since, like my brothers, I was privately educated, I had no diplomas or similar records to show them, and they had to give me an equivalency examination in their place. Evidently I did quite well, for I was immediately accepted. I wired Mother, who sent a check for $3,000 to cover my first year's tuition and expenses.

I enrolled as a History major; among my first-year courses were Medieval English Constitutional History and the Survey of Western Historical Currents; naturally, my marks were the highest in the class in both cases. I worked diligently and even with a sort of frenzied fury. My other courses, in the sciences or in the arts, I devoted no more nor no less time to than was necessary, but history was my ruling passion.

At least, through my first two semesters of college.

June came, and final exam, and then I returned to Wisconsin, where Mother was waiting. It was June 21 when I returned; since not all colleges end their spring semester simultaneously, some of my brothers had been home for more than a week, others had not yet arrived. Richard had sent word that he was in Los Angeles, and would be with us after the first of July. Mark had signed a baseball contract and was pitching for a team in New Mexico, and he, too, would not be with us.

The summer passed rapidly.

We spent it as we had in the old days before college, sharing our individual specialties, talking, meeting regularly and privately with Mother to discuss the goals that still lay ahead. Except for Claude and George, we had scattered in different directions, no two of us at the same school.

I returned to Princeton that fall, for my sophomore year. It passed, and I made the homeward journey again, and in the fall traveled once more eastward. The junior year went by likewise.

And I began to detect signs of a curious change in my inward self. It was a change I did not dare mention to Mother, on those July days when I met with her in her room near the library. I did not tell my brothers, either. I kept my knowledge to myself, brooding over it, wondering

70

why it was that this thing should happen to me, why I should be singled out.

For I was discovering that the study of history bored me utterly and completely.

The spirit of rebellion grew in me during my final year in college. My marks had been excellent; I had achieved Phi Beta Kappa and several graduate schools were interested in having me continue my studies with them. But I had been speaking to a few chosen friends (none of whom knew my bizarre family background, of course) and my values had been slowly shifting.

I realized that I had mined history as deeply as I ever cared to. Waking and sleeping, for more than fifteen years, I had pondered Waterloo and Bunker Hill, considered the personalities of Cromwell and James II, held imaginary conversations with Jefferson and Augustus Caesar and Charles Martel.

And I was bored with it.

It began to become evident to others, eventually. One day during my final semester a friend asked me, "Is there something worrying you, Harry?"

I shook my head quickly—*too* quickly. "No," I said. "Why? Do I look worried?"

"You look worse than worried. You look obsessed."

We laughed about it, and finally we went down to the student center and had a few beers, and before long my tongue had loosened a little.

I said, "There *is* something worrying me. And you know what it is? I'm afraid I won't live up to the standards my family set for me."

Guffaws greeted me. "Come off it, Harry! Phi Beta in your junior year, top class standing, a brilliant career in history ahead of you—what do they want from you, blood?"

I chuckled and gulped my beer and mumbled something innocuous, but inside I was curdling.

71

Everything I was, I owed to Mother. She made me what I am. But I was played out, as a student of history; I was the family failure, the goat, the rotten egg. Raymond still wrestled gleefully with nuclear physics, with Heisenberg and Schrodinger and the others. Mark gloried in his fast ball and his slider and his curve. Paul daubed canvas merrily in his Greenwich Village flat near NYU, and even Robert seemed to take delight in keeping books.

Only I had failed. History had become repugnant to me. I was in rebellion against it. I would disappoint my mother, become the butt of my brothers' scorn, and live in despair, hating the profession of historian and fitted by training for nothing else.

I was graduated from Princeton summa cum laude, a few days after my twenty-first birthday. I wired Mother that I was on my way home, and bought train tickets.

It was a long and grueling journey to Wisconsin. I spent my time thinking, trying to choose between the unpleasant alternatives that faced me.

I could attempt duplicity, telling my mother I was still studying history, while actually preparing myself for some more attractive profession—the law, perhaps.

I could confess to her at once my failure of purpose, ask her forgiveness for disappointing her and flawing her grand scheme, and try to begin afresh in another field.

Or I could forge ahead with history, compelling myself grimly to take an interest, cramping and paining myself so that my mother's design would be complete.

None of them seemed desirable paths to take. I brooded over it, and was weary and apprehensive by the time I arrived at our farm.

The first of my brothers I saw was Mark. He sat on the front porch of the big house, reading a book which I recognized at once and with some surprise as Volume I of Churchill. He looked up at me and smiled feebly.

I frowned. "I didn't expect to find *you* here, Mark. According to the local sports pages the Braves are playing on the Coast this week. How come you're not with them?"

His voice was a low murmur. "Because they gave me my release," he said.

"What?"

He nodded. "I'm washed up at twenty-one. They made me a free agent; that means I can hook up with any team that wants me."

"And you're just taking a little rest before offering yourself around?"

He shook his head. "I'm through. Kaput. Harry, I just can't stand baseball. It's a silly, stupid game. You know how many times I had to stand out there in baggy knickers and throw a bit of horsehide at some jerk with a club in his paws? A hundred, hundred-fifty times a game, every four days. For what? What the hell does it all mean? Why should I bother?"

There was a strange gleam in his eyes. I said, "Have you told Mother?"

"I don't dare! She thinks I'm on leave or something. Harry, how can I tell her—"

"I know." Briefly, I told him of my own disenchantment with history. We were mutually delighted to learn that we were not alone in our affliction. I picked up my suitcase, scrambled up the steps, and went inside.

Dewey was cleaning up the common room as I passed through. He nodded hello glumly. I said, "How's the tooth trade?"

He whirled and glared at me viciously.

"Something wrong?" I asked.

"I've been accepted by four dental schools, Harry."

"Is that any cause for misery?"

He let the broom drop, walked over to me, and whispered, "I'll murder you if you tell Mother this. But the thought of spending my life poking around in foul-smelling oral cavities sickens me. *Sickens*."

"But I thought—"

"Yeah. You thought. You've got it soft; you just need to dig books out of the library and rearrange what they say and call it new research. I have to drill and clean and fill and plug and—" He stopped. "Harry, I'll kill you if you breathe a word of this. I don't want Mother to know that I didn't come out the way she wanted."

I repeated what I had said to Mark—and told him about Mark, for good measure. Then I made my way upstairs to my old room. I felt a burden lifting from me; I was not alone. At least two of my brothers felt the same way. I wondered how many more were at last rebelling against the disciplines of a lifetime.

Poor Mother, I thought! Poor Mother!

Our first family council of the summer was held that night. Stephen and Saul were the last to arrive, Stephen resplendent in his Annapolis garb, Saul crisp looking and stiff-backed from West Point. Mother had worked hard to wangle appointments for those two.

We sat around the big table and chatted. The first phase of our lives, Mother told us, had ended. Now, our preliminary educations were complete, and we would undertake the final step toward our professions—those of us who had not already entered them.

Mother looked radiant that evening, tall, energetic, her white hair cropped mannishly short, as she sat about the table with her thirty-one strapping sons. I envied and pitied her: envied her for the sweet serenity of her life, which had proceeded so inexorably and without swerve toward the goal of her experiment, and pitied her for the disillusioning that awaited her.

For Mark and Dewey and I were not the only failures in the crop.

I had made discreet enquiries, during the day. I learned

74

that Anthony found literary criticism to be a fraud and a sham, that Paul knew clearly he had no talent as a painter (and, also, that very few of his contemporaries did either), that Robert bitterly resented a career of bookkeeping, that piano playing hurt George's fingers, that Claude had had difficulty with his composing because he was tone deaf, that the journalistic grind was too strenuous for Jonas, that John longed to quit the seminarial life because he had no calling, that Albert hated the uncertain bohemianism of an actor's life—

We circulated, all of us raising for the first time the question that had sprouted in our minds during the past several years. I made the astonishing discovery that not one of Donna Mitchell's sons cared for the career that had been chosen for him.

The experiment had been a resounding flop.

Late that evening, after Mother had gone to bed, we remained together, discussing our predicament. How could we tell her? How could we destroy her life's work? And yet, how could we compel ourselves to lives of unending drudgery?

Robert wanted to study engineering; Barry, to write. I realized I cared much more for law than for history, while Leonard longed to exchange law for the physical sciences. James, our banker-manque, much preferred politics. And so it went, with Richard (who claimed five robberies, a rape, and innumerable picked pockets) pouring out his desire to settle down and live within the law as an honest farmer.

It was pathetic.

Summing up the problem in his neat forensic way, Leonard said, "Here's our dilemma. Do we all keep quiet about this and ruin our lives, or do we speak up and ruin Mother's experiment?"

"I think we ought to continue as is, for the time being,"

Saul said. "Perhaps Mother will die in the next year or two. We can start over then."

"Perhaps she *doesn't* die?" Edward wanted to know. "She's tough as nails. She may last another twenty or thirty or even forty years."

"And we're past twenty-one already," remarked Raymond. "If we hang on too long at what we're doing, it'll be too late to change. You can't start studying for a new profession when you're thirty-five."

"Maybe we'll get to *like* what we're doing by then," suggested David hopefully. "Diplomatic service isn't as bad as all that, and I'd say—"

"What about me," Paul yelped. "I can't paint and I know I can't paint. I've got nothing but starvation ahead of me unless I wise up and get into business in a hurry. You want me to keep messing up good white canvas the rest of my life?"

"It won't work," said Barry, in a doleful voice. "We'll have to tell her."

Douglas shook his head. "We can't do that. You know just what she'll do. She'll bring down the umpteen volumes of notes she's made on this experiment, and ask us if we're going to let it all come to naught."

"He's right," Albert said. "I can picture the scene now. The big organ-pipe voice blasting us for our lack of faith, the accusations of ingratitude—"

"Ingratitude?" William shouted. "She twisted us and pushed us and molded us without asking our permission. Hell, she *created* us with her laboratory tricks. But that didn't give her the right to make zombies out of us."

"Still," Martin said, "we can't just go to her and tell her that it's all over. The shock would kill her."

"Well?" Richard asked in the silence that followed. "What's wrong with that?"

For a moment, no one spoke. The house was quiet; we heard footsteps descending the stairs. We froze.

76

Mother appeared, an imperial figure even in her old housecoat. "You boys are kicking up too much of a racket down here," she boomed. "I know you're glad to see each other again after a year, but I need my sleep."

She turned and strode upstairs again. We heard her bedroom door slam shut. For an instant we were all ten-year-olds again, diligently studying our books for fear of Mother's displeasure.

I moistened my lips. "Well?" I asked. "I call for a vote on Richard's suggestion."

Martin, as a chemist, prepared the drink, using Donald's medical advice as his guide. Saul, Stephen, and Raymond dug a grave, in the woods at the back of our property. Douglas and Mark built the coffin.

Richard, ending his criminal career with a murder to which we were all accessories before the fact, carried the fatal beverage upstairs to Mother the next morning, and persuaded her to sip it. One sip was all that was necessary; Martin had done his work well.

Leonard offered us a legal opinion: It was justifiable homicide. We placed the body in its coffin and carried it out across the fields. Richard, Peter, Jonas, and Charles were her pallbearers; the others of us followed in their path.

We lowered the body into the ground and John said a few words over her. Then, slowly, we closed over the grave and replaced the sod, and began the walk back to the house.

"She died happy," Anthony said. "She never suspected the size of her failure." It was her epitaph.

As our banker, James supervised the division of her assets, which were considerable, into thirty-one equal parts. Noel composed a short fragment of prose which we agreed summed up our sentiments.

We left the farm that night, scattering in every direction, anxious to begin life. All that went before was a dream from which we now awakened. We agreed to meet at the farm each year, on the anniversary of her death, in memory of the woman who had so painstakingly divided a zygote into thirty-two viable cells, and who had spent a score of years conducting an experiment based on a theory that had proven to be utterly false.

We felt no regret, no qualm. We had done what needed to be done, and on that last day some of us had finally functioned in the professions for which Mother had intended us.

I, too. My first and last work of history will be this, an account of Mother and her experiment, which records the beginning and the end of her work. And now it is complete.

THE SHADOW OF WINGS

The children came running towards him, laughing and shouting, up from the lakeside to the spot on the grassy hill where he lay reading; and as Dr. John Donaldson saw what was clutched in the hand of his youngest son, he felt an involuntary tremor of disgust.

"Look, John! Look what Paul caught!" That was his oldest, Joanne. She was nine, a brunette rapidly growing tan on this vacation trip. Behind her came David, eight, fair-haired and lobster-skinned, and in the rear was Paul, the six-year-old, out of breath and gripping in his still pudgy hand a small green frog.

Donaldson shoved his book—Haley, *Studies in Morphological Linguistics*—to one side and sat up. Paul thrust the frog almost into his face. "I saw it hop, John—and I caught it!" He pantomimed the catch with his free hand.

"I saw him do it," affirmed David.

The frog's head projected between thumb and first finger; two skinny webbed feet dangled free at the other end of Paul's hand, while the middle of the unfortunate batrachian was no doubt being painfully compressed by the small clammy hand. Donaldson felt pleased by Paul's display of coordination, unusual for a six-year-old. But at the same time he wished the boy would take the poor frog back to the lake and let it go.

"Paul," he started to say, "you really ought to—"

The direct-wave phone at the far end of the blanket

bleeped, indicating that Martha, back at the bungalow, was calling.

"It's Mommy," Joanne said. Somehow they had never cared to call her by her first name, as they did him. "See what she wants, John."

Donaldson sprawled forward and activated the phone. "Martha?"

"John, there's a phone call for you from Washington. I told them you were down by the lake, but they say it's important and they'll hold on."

Donaldson frowned. "Who from Washington?"

"Caldwell, he said. Bureau of Extraterrestrial Affairs. Said it was urgent."

Sighing, Donaldson said, "Okay, I'm coming."

He looked at Joanne and said, as if she hadn't heard the conversation at all, "There's a call for me and I have to go to the cottage to take it. Make sure your brothers don't go into the water while I'm gone. And see that Paul lets that confounded frog go."

Picking up his book, he levered himself to his feet and set out for the phone in the bungalow at a brisk trot.

Caldwell's voice was crisp and efficient and not at all apologetic as he said, "I'm sorry to have to interrupt you during your vacation, Dr. Donaldson. But it's an urgent matter and they tell us you're the man who can help us."

"Perhaps I am. Just exactly what is it you want?"

"Check me if I'm wrong on the background. You're professor of Linguistics at Columbia, a student of the Kethlani languages and author of a study of Kethlani linguistics published in 2087."

"Yes, yes, that's all correct. But—"

"Dr. Donaldson, we've captured a live Kethlan. He entered the System in a small ship and one of our patrol vessels grappled him in, ship and all. We've got him here

80

in Washington and we want you to come talk to him."

For an instant Donaldson was too stunned to react. A live Kethlan? That was like saying, We've found a live Sumerian, or, We've found a live Etruscan.

The Kethlani languages were precise, neat and utterly dead. At one time in the immeasurable past the Kethlani had visited the Solar System. They had left records of their visit on Mars and Venus, in two languages. One of the languages was translatable, because the Martians had translated it into their own, and the Martian language was still spoken as it had been a hundred thousand years before.

Donaldson had obtained his doctorate with what was hailed as a brilliant Rosetta Stone type analysis of the Kethlani language. But a *live* Kethlan? Why—

After a moment he realized he was staring stupidly at his unevenly tanned face in the mirror above the phone cabinet, and that the man on the other end of the wire was making impatient noises.

Slowly he said, "I can be in Washington this afternoon, I guess. Give me some time to pack up my things. You won't want me for long, will you?"

"Until we're through talking to the Kethlan," Caldwell said.

"All right," Donaldson said. "I can take a vacation any time. Kethlani don't come along that often."

He hung up and peered at his face in the mirror. He had had curly reddish hair once, but fifteen years of the academic life had worn his forehead bare. His eyes were mild, his nose narrow and unemphatic, his lips thin and pale. As he studied himself, he did not think he looked very impressive. He looked professional. That was to be expected.

"Well?" Martha asked.

Donaldson shrugged. "They captured some kind of alien spaceship with a live one aboard. And it seems I'm the

81

only person who can speak the language. They want me right away."

"You're going?"

"Of course. It shouldn't take more than a few days. You can manage with the children by yourself, can't you? I mean—"

She smiled faintly, walked around behind him and kneaded the muscle of his sun-reddened back in an affectionate gesture. "I know better than to argue," she said. "We can take a vacation next year."

He swiveled his left hand behind his back, caught her hand and squeezed it fondly. He knew she would never object. After all, his happiness was her happiness—and he was never happier than when working in his chosen field. The phone call today would probably lead to all sorts of unwanted and unneeded publicity for him. But it would also bring him academic success, and there was no denying the genuine thrill of finding out how accurate his guesses about Kethlani pronunciation were.

"You'd better go down to the lake and get the children," he said. "I'll want to say good-bye before I leave."

They had the ship locked in a stasis field in the basement of the Bureau of ET Affairs Building, on Constitution Avenue just across from the National Academy of Sciences. The great room looked like nothing so much as a crypt, Donaldson thought as he entered. Beam projectors were mounted around the walls, focusing a golden glow on the ship. Caught it the field, the ship hovered in midair, a slim, strange-looking torpedolike object about forty feet long and ten feet across the thickest space. A tingle rippled up Donaldson's spine as he saw the Kethlani cursives painted in blue along the hull. He translated them reflexively: *Bringer of Friendship*.

"That's how we knew it was a Kethlani ship," Caldwell said, at his side. He was a small, intense man who hardly reached Donaldson's shoulder; he was Associate Director of the Bureau, and in his superior's absence he was running the show.

Donaldson indicated the projectors. "How come the gadgetry? Couldn't you just sit the ship on the floor instead of floating it that way?"

"That ship's heavy," Caldwell said. "Might crack the floor. Anyway, it's easier to maneuver this way. We can raise or lower the ship, turn it, float it in or out of the door."

"I see," Donaldson said. "And you say there's a live Kethlan in there?"

Caldwell nodded. He jerked a thumb toward a miniature broadcasting station at the far end of the big room. "We've been in contact with him. He talks to us and we talk to him. But we don't understand a damned bit of it, of course. You want to try?"

Donaldson shook his head up and down in a tense affirmative. Caldwell led him down to the radio set, where an eager-looking young man in military uniform sat making adjustments.

Caldwell said, "This is Dr. Donaldson of Columbia. He wrote the definitive book on Kethlani languages. He wants to talk to our friend in there."

A microphone was thrust into Donaldson's hands. He looked at it blankly, then at the pink face of the uniformed man, then at the ship. The inscription was in Kethlani A language, for which Donaldson was grateful. There were two Kethlani languages, highly dissimilar, which he had labeled A and B. He knew his way around in A well enough, but his mastery of Kethlani B was still exceedingly imperfect.

"How do I use this thing?"

"You push the button on the handle, and talk. That's all. The Kethlan can hear you. Anything he says will be picked up here." He indicated a tape recorder and a speaker on the table.

Donaldson jabbed down on the button, and, feeling a strange sense of disorientation, uttered two words in greeting in Kethlani A.

The pronunciation, of course, was sheer guesswork. Donaldson had worked out what was to him a convincing Kethlani phonetic system, but whether that bore any relation to fact remained to be seen.

He waited a moment. Then the speaker emitted a series of harsh, unfamiliar sounds—and, buried in them like gems in a kitchen midden, Donaldson detected familiar-sounding words.

"Speak slowly," he said in Kethlani A. "I . . . have only a few words."

The reply came about ten seconds later, in more measured accents. "How . . . do . . . you . . . speak our language?"

Donaldson fumbled in his small vocabulary for some way of explaining that he had studied Kethlani documents left behind on Mars centuries earlier, and compared them with their understandable Martian translations until he had pried some sense out of them.

He glimpsed the pale, sweat-beaded faces of the ET men around him; they were mystified, wondering what he was saying to the alien but not daring to interrupt. Donaldson felt a flash of pity for them. Until today the bureau had concerned itself with petty things: import of Martian antiquities, study visas for Venus, and the like. Now, suddenly, they found themselves staring at an extra-solar spaceship, and all the giant problems that entailed.

"Find out why he came to the Solar System," Caldwell whispered.

"I'm trying to," Donaldson murmured with some irritation. He said in Kethlani, "You have made a long journey."

"Yes . . . and alone."

"Why have you come?"

There was a long moment of silence; Donaldson waited, feeling tension of crackling intensity starting to build within him. The unreality of the situation obsessed him. He had been fondly confident that he would never have the opportunity to speak actual Kethlani, and that confidence was being shattered.

Finally: "I . . . have come . . . why?"

The inversion was grammatically correct. "Yes," Donaldson said. "Why?"

Another long pause. Then the alien said something which Donaldson did not immediately understand. He asked for a repeat.

It made little sense—but, of course, his Kethlani vocabulary was a shallow one, and he had additional difficulty in comprehending because he had made some mistakes in interpreting vowel values when constructing his Kethlani phonetics.

But the repeat came sharp and clear, and there was no mistaking it.

"I do . . . do not like to talk in this way. Come inside my ship and we will talk there."

"What's he saying?" Caldwell prodded.

Shaken, Donaldson let the mike dangle from limp fingers. "He—he says he wants me to come inside the ship. He doesn't like long-distance conversations."

Caldwell turned at a right angle and said to a waiting assistant. "All right. Have Matthews reverse the stasis field and lower the ship. We're going to give the Kethlan some company."

Donaldson blinked. "Company? You mean you're sending me in there?"

"I sure as hell do mean that. The Kethlan said it's the only way he'd talk, didn't he? And that's what you're

85

here for. To talk to him. So why shouldn't you go in there, eh?"

"Well—look, Caldwell, suppose it isn't safe?"

"If I thought it was risky, I wouldn't send you in," Caldwell said blandly.

Donaldson shook his head. "But look—I don't want to seem cowardly, but I've got three children to think about. I'm not happy about facing an alien being inside his own ship, if you get me."

"I get you," said Caldwell tiredly. "All right. You want to go home? You want to call the whole business off right here and now?"

"Of course not. But—"

"But then you'll have to go in."

"How will I be able to breathe?"

"The alien air is close enough to our own. He's used to more carbon dioxide and less oxygen, but he can handle our air. There's no problem. And no risk. We had a man in there yesterday when the Kethlan opened the outer lock. You won't be in any physical danger. The alien won't bother you."

"I hope not," Donaldson said. He felt hesitant about it; he hadn't bargained on going inside any extra solar spaceships. But they were clustered impatiently around him, waiting to send him inside, and he didn't seem to have much choice. He sensed a certain contempt for him on their faces already. He didn't want to increase their distaste.

"Will you go in?" Caldwell asked.

"All right. All right. Yes. I'll go in."

Nervously Donaldson picked up the microphone and clamped a cold finger over the control button.

"Open your lock," he said to the alien being. "I'm coming inside."

There was a moment's delay while the stasis field projectors were reversed, lowering the ship gently to floor

86

level. As soon as it touched, a panel in the gleaming golden side of the ship rolled smoothly open, revealing an inner panel.

Donaldson moistened his lips, handed the microphone to Caldwell and walked uncertainly forward. He reached the lip of the airlock, stepped up over it and into the ship. Immediately the door rolled shut behind him, closing him into a chamber about seven feet high and four feet wide, bordered in front and back by the outer and inner doors of the lock.

He waited. Had he been claustrophobic he would have been hysterical by now. *But I never would have come in here in the first place then,* he thought.

He waited. More than a minute passed; then, finally, the blank wall before him rolled aside, and the ship was open to him at last. He entered.

At first it seemed to him the interior was totally dark. Gradually, his retinal rods conveyed a little information.

A dim light flickered at one end of the narrow tubular ship. He could make out a few things: rows of reinforcing struts circling the ship at regularly spaced distances; a kind of control panel with quite thoroughly alien-looking instruments on it; a large chamber at one end which might be used for storage of food.

But where's the alien? Donaldson wondered.

He turned, slowly, through a three hundred sixty degree rotation, squinting in the dimness. A sort of mist hung before his eyes; the alien's exhalation, perhaps. But he saw no sign of the Kethlan. There was a sweetish, musky odor in the ship, unpleasant though not unbearable.

"Everything okay?" Caldwell's voice said in his earphones.

"So far. But I can't find the alien. It's damnably dark in here."

"Look up," Caldwell advised. "You'll find him. Took our man a while too, yesterday.'

Puzzled, Donaldson raised his head and stared into the gloom-shrouded rafters of the ship, wondering what he was supposed to see. In Kethlani he said loudly, "Where are you? I see you not?"

"I am here," came the harsh voice, from above.

Donaldson looked. Then he backed away, double-taking, and looked again.

A great shaggy thing hung head down against the roof of the ship. Staring intently, Donaldson made out a blunt, piggish face with flattened nostrils and huge flaring ears; the eyes, bright yellow but incredibly tiny, glittered with the unmistakable light of intelligence. He saw a body about the size of a man, covered with darkish thick fur and terminating in two short, thick, powerful-looking legs. As he watched the Kethlan shivered and stretched forth its vast leathery wings. In the darkness, Donaldson could see the corded muscular arm in the wing, and the very human looking fingers which sprouted from the uppermost part of the wing.

Violent disgust rose in him, compounded from his own general dislike for animals and from the half-remembered Transylvanian folktales that formed part of every child's heritage. He felt sick; he controlled himself only by remembering that he was in essence an ambassador, and any sickness would have disastrous consequences for him and for Earth. He dared not offend the Kethlan.

My God, he thought. *An intelligent bat!*

He managed to stammer out the words for greeting, and the alien responded. Donaldson, looking away, saw the elongated shadow of wings cast across the ship by the faint light at the other end. He felt weak, wobbly-legged; he wanted desperately to dash through the now-closed airlock. But he forced himself to recover balance. He had a job to do.

"I did not expect you to know Kethlani," the alien said. "It makes my job much less difficult."

88

"And your job is—?"

"To bring friendship from my people to yours. To link our worlds in brotherhood."

The last concept was a little muddy to Donaldson; the literal translation he made mentally was *children-of-one cave*, but some questioning eventually brought over the concept of brotherhood.

His eyes were growing more accustomed to the lighting, now, and he could see the Kethlan fairly well. An ugly brute, no doubt of it—but probably I look just as bad to him, he thought. The creature's wingspread was perhaps seven or eight feet. Donaldson tried to picture a world of the beasts, skies thick with leather-winged commuters on their way to work.

Evolution had made numerous modifications in the bat structure, Donaldson saw. The brain, of course; and the extra fingers, aside from the ones from which the wings had sprouted. The eyes looked weak, in typical bat fashion, but probably there was compensation by way of keen auditory senses.

Donaldson said, "Where is your world?"

"Far from here. It —"

The rest of the answer was unintelligible to Donaldson. He felt savage impatience with his own limited vocabulary; he wished he had worked just a little harder on translating the Syrtis Major documents. Well, it was too late for that now, of course.

Caldwell cut in suddenly from outside. "Well? We're picking up all the jabber. What's all the talk about?"

"Can't you wait till I'm finished?" Donaldson snapped. Then, repenting, he said: "Sorry. Guess I'm jumpy. Seems he's an ambassador from his people, trying to establish friendly relations with us. At least, I think so. I'll tell you more when I know something about it."

Slowly, in fits and starts, the story emerged. Frequently Donaldson had to ask the Kethlan to stop and double

89

back while he puzzled over a word. He had no way of recording any of the new words he was learning, but he had always had a good memory, and he simply tucked them away.

The Kethlani had visited the Solar System many years ago. Donaldson was unable to translate the actual figure, but it sounded like a lot. At that time the Martians were at the peak of their civilization, and Earth was just an untamed wilderness populated by naked primates. The Kethlan wryly admitted that they had written off Earth as a potential place of civilization because a study of the bat population of Earth had proved unpromising. They had never expected the primates to evolve this way.

But now they had returned, thousands of years later. Mars was bleak and its civilization decayed, but the third world had unexpectedly attained a high degree of culture and was welcome to embrace the Kethlani worlds in friendship and amity.

"How many worlds do you inhabit?"

The Kethlan counted to fifteen by ones. "There are many others we do not inhabit, but simply maintain friendly relations with. Yours would be one, we hope."

The conversation seemed to dwindle to a halt. Donaldson had run out of questions to ask, and he was exhausted by the hour-long strain of conversing in an alien language, under these conditions, within a cramped ship, talking to a creature whose physical appearance filled him with loathing and fear.

His head throbbed. His stomach was knotted in pain and sweat made his clothes cling clammily to his body. He started to grope for ways to terminate the interview; then an idea struck him.

He quoted a fragment of a document written in pure Kethlani B.

There was an instant of stunned silence; then the

alien asked in tones of unmistakable suspicion, "Where did you learn that language?"

"I haven't really learned it. I just know a few words."

He explained that he had found examples of both Kethlani A and Kethlani B along with their Martian equivalents; he had worked fairly comprehensively on the A language, but had only begun to explore the B recently.

The Kethlan seemed to accept that. Then it said: "That is not a Kethlani language."

Surprised, Donaldson uttered the interrogative expletive.

The Kethlan said, "It is the language of our greatest enemies, our rivals, our bitter foes. It is the Thygnor tongue."

"But—why did we find your language and the other side by side, then?"

After a long pause the alien said, "Once Thygnor and Kethlan were friends. Long ago we conducted a joint expedition to this sector of space. Long ago, before the rivalry sprang up. But now—" the alien took on a sorrowful inflection—"now we are enemies."

That explained a great many things, Donaldson realized. The differences between Kethlani A and Kethlani B had been too great for it to seem as if one race spoke both of them. But a joint expedition—that made it understandable.

"Some day, perhaps, the Thygnor will visit your world. But by then you will be on guard against them."

"What do they look like?"

The alien described them, and Donaldson listened and was revolted. As far as he could understand, they were giant intelligent toads, standing erect, amphibian but warm-blooded, vile-smelling, their bodies exuding a nauseous thick secretion.

Giant toads, bats, the lizards of Mars—evidently the primate monopoly of intelligence was confined solely to Earth, Donaldson realized. It was a humbling thought.

His face wrinkled in displeasure at the mental image of the toad people the Kethlan had created for him, as he recalled the harmless little frog Paul had captured by the lake.

He spoke in English, attracting Caldwell's attention, and explained the situation.

"He wants me to swear brotherhood with him. He also says there's another intelligent race with interstellar travel —toads, no less—and that they're likely to pay us a visit some day too. What should I do?"

"Go ahead and swear brotherhood," Caldwell said after a brief pause. "It can't hurt. We can always unswear it later, if we like. Say we had our fingers crossed while we were doing it, or something. Then when the frogs get here we can find out which bunch is better for us to be in league with."

The cynicism of the reply annoyed Donaldson, but it was not his place to raise any objections. He said to the alien, "I am prepared to pledge brotherhood between Earth and the Kethlan worlds."

The Kethlan fluttered suddenly down from its perch with a rustle of great wings, and stood facing Donaldson, tucking its wings around its thick shaggy body. Alarmed, Donaldson stepped back.

The alien said reassuringly, "The way we pledge is by direct physical embrace, symbolizing harmony and friendship across the cosmos." He unfurled his wings. "Come close to me."

No! Donaldson shrieked inwardly, as the mighty wings rose high and wrapped themselves about him. *Go away! Don't touch me!* He could smell the sweet, musky smell of the alien, feel its furry warmth, hear the mighty heart pounding, pounding in that massive rib cage. . . .

Revulsion dizzied him. He forced himself to wrap his arms around the barrel of a body while the wings blanketed him, and they stood that way for a moment, locked in a tight embrace.

At length the alien released him. "Now we are friends. It is only the beginning of a long and fruitful relationship between our peoples. I hope to speak with you again before long."

It was a dismissal. On watery legs Donaldson tottered forward toward the opening airlock, pausing only to mutter a word of farewell before he stumbled through and out into the arms of the waiting men outside.

"Well?" Caldwell demanded. "What happened? Did you swear brotherhood?"

"Yes," Donaldson said wearily. "I swore." The stench of the alien clung to him, sweet in his nostrils. It was as though throbbing wings still enfolded him. "I'm leaving now," he said. "I still have a little of my vacation left. I want to take it."

He gulped a drink that someone handed him. He was shaking and gray-faced, but the effect of the embrace was wearing off. *Only an irrational phobia,* he told himself. *I shouldn't be reacting this way.*

But already he was beginning to forget the embrace of the Kethlani, and the rationalization did him no good. A new and more dreadful thought was beginning to develop within him.

He was the only Terrestrial expert on Kethlani B, too— the Thygnor tongue. And some day, perhaps soon, the Thygnor were going to come to Earth, and Caldwell was going to impress him into service as an interpreter again.

He wondered how the toad people pledged eternal brotherhood.

ABSOLUTELY INFLEXIBLE

The detector over in one corner of Mahler's little office gleamed a soft red. With a weary gesture of his hand he drew it to the attention of the sad-eyed time jumper who sat slouched glumly across the desk from him, looking cramped and uncomfortable in his bulky spacesuit.

"You see," Mahler said, tapping his desk. "They've just found another one. We're constantly bombarded with you people. When you get to the Moon, you'll find a whole Dome full of them. I've sent over four thousand there myself since I took over the bureau. And that was over eight years ago—in twenty-seven twenty-six, to be exact. An average of five hundred a year. Hardly a day goes by without someone dropping in on us."

"And not one has been set free," the time jumper said. "Every time traveler who's come here has been packed off to the Moon immediately. Every single one."

"Every one," Mahler agreed. He peered through the thick shielding, trying to see what sort of man was hidden inside the spacesuit.

Mahler aften wondered about the men he condemned so easily to the Moon. This one was small of stature, with wispy locks of white hair pasted to his high forehead by perspiration. Evidently he had been a scientist, a respected man of his time, perhaps a happy father—although very few of the time jumpers were family men. Perhaps he possessed some bit of scientific knowledge which would be invaluable to the 28th Century. Or perhaps he didn't. It scarcely mattered. Like all the rest, he would have to be sent to the Moon, to live out his remaining days under the grueling, primitive conditions of the Dome.

"Don't you think that's a little cruel?" the other asked. "I came here with no malice, no intent to harm anyone. I'm simply a scientific observer from the past. Driven by curiosity, I took the Jump. I never expected that I'd be walking into life imprisonment."

"I'm sorry," Mahler said, getting up.

He decided to end the interview then and there. He had to get rid of this jumper because there was another space traveler coming right up. Some days they came thick and fast, and this looked like one of the really bad days. But the efficient mechanical tracers never missed a jumper.

"But can't I live on Earth and stay in this spacesuit?" the man asked, panicky now that he saw his interview with Mahler was coming to an end. "That way I'd be sealed off from contact at all times."

"Please don't make this any harder than it is for me," Mahler said. "I've explained to you why we must be absolutely inflexible. There cannot—must not—be any exceptions. Two centuries have now passed since the last outbreak of disease on Earth. So naturally we've lost most of the resistance acquired over the countless generations when disease was rampant. I'm risking my life coming so close to you, even with the spacesuit sealing you off."

Mahler signaled to the tall, powerful guards who were waiting in the corridor, looking like huge, heavily armored beetles in the casings that protected them from infection. This was always the worst moment.

"Look," Mahler said, frowning with impatience. "You're a walking death trap. You probably carry enough disease germs to kill half the world. Even a cold—a *common* cold—would wipe out millions now. Acquired immunity to disease has simply vanished over the past two centuries. It's no longer needed, with all diseases conquered. But you time travelers show up loaded with potentialities for all the diseases that once wiped out whole populations. And we can't risk having you stay here with them."

"But I'd—"

"I know. You'd swear by all that's holy to you or to me that you'd never leave the confines of the spacesuit. Sorry. The word of the most honorable man doesn't carry any weight against the safety of two billion human lives. We can't take the slightest risk by letting you stay on Earth.

"I know. It's unfair, it's cruel—it's anything else you may choose to call it. You had no idea you would walk into a situation like this. Well, I feel sorry for you. But you knew you were going on a one-way trip to the future, and would be subject to whatever that future might decide to do with you. You knew that you could not possibly return in time to your own age."

Mahler began to tidy up the paper on his desk with a brusqueness that signaled finality. "I'm terribly sorry, but you'll just have to try to understand our point of view," he said. "We're frightened to death by your very presence here. We can't allow you to roam Earth, even in a spacesuit. No. There's nothing for you but the Moon. I have to be absolutely inflexible. Take him away," he said gesturing to the guards.

They advanced on the little man and began gently to ease him out of Mahler's office.

Mahler sank gratefully into the pneumochair and sprayed his throat with laryngogel. These long speeches always left him exhausted, and now his throat felt raw and scraped. *Someday I'll get throat cancer from all this talking*, Mahler thought. *And that'll mean the nuisance*

96

of an operation. But if I don't do this job, someone else will have to.

Mahler heard the protesting screams of the time jumper impassively. In the beginning he had been ready to resign on first witnessing the inevitable frenzied reaction of jumper after jumper as the guards dragged them away. But eight years had hardened him.

They had given him the job because he had been a hard man in the first place. It was a job that called for a hard man. Condrin, his predecessor, had not been the same sort of man at all, and because of his tragic weakness Condrin was now himself on the Moon. He had weakened after heading the bureau a year, and had let a jumper go.

The jumper had promised to secrete himself at the tip of Antarctica and Condrin, thinking that Antarctica would be as safe as the Moon, had foolishly released him. Right after that they had called Mahler in. In eight years Mahler had sent four thousand men to the Moon. The first had been the runaway jumper—intercepted in Buenos Aires after he had left a trail of disease down the hemisphere from Appalachia to the Argentine Protectorate. The second had been Condrin.

It was getting to be a tiresome job, Mahler thought. But he was proud to hold it and be in a position to save millions of lives. It took a strong man to do what he was doing. He leaned back and awaited the arrival of the next jumper.

Instead, the door slid smoothly open, and the burly body of Dr. Fournet, the bureau's chief medical man, broke the photoelectric beam. Mahler glanced up. Fournet carried a time rig dangling from one hand.

"I took this away from our latest customer," Fournet said. "He told the medic who examined him that it was a two-way rig, and I thought you'd better be the first to look it over."

Mahler came to full attention quickly. A two-way rig? Unlikely, he thought. But if it was true it would mean the end of the dreary jumper prison on the Moon. Only how could a two-way rig exist? He reached out and took the rig from Fournet.

"It seems to be a conventional twenty-fourth century type," he said.

"But notice the extra dial," Fournet said, frowning.

Mahler peered and nodded. "Yes. It *seems* to be a two-way rig, all right. But how can we test it? And it's not really very probable," he added. "Why should a two-way rig suddenly show up from the twenty-fourth century, when no other traveler has one? We don't even have two-way time travel ourselves, and our scientists insist that we never will.

"Still," he mused, "it's a nice thing to dream about. We'll have to study this a little more closely. But I don't seriously think it will work. Bring the jumper in, will you?"

As Fournet turned to signal the guards, Mahler asked him, "What's the man's medical report, by the way?"

"From here to here," Fournet said somberly. "You name it, he's carrying it. Better get him shipped off to the Moon as quickly as you can. I won't feel safe until he's off this planet."

The big medic waved to the guards.

Mahler smiled. Fournet's overcautiousness was proverbial in the Bureau. Even if a jumper were to show up completely free from disease, Fournet would probably insist that he was carrying everything from asthma to leprosy.

The guards brought the jumper into Mahler's office. He was fairly tall, Mahler saw—and quite young. It was difficult to see his face clearly through the dim plate of the protective spacesuit which all jumpers were compelled to wear. But Mahler could tell that the young time traveler's face had much of the lean, hard look of Mahler's own. It was just possible that the jumper's eyes had widened in surprise as he entered the office, but Mahler could not be sure.

"I never dreamed I'd find *you* here," the jumper said. The transmitter of the spacesuit brought the young man's voice over deeply and resonantly. "Your name is Mahler, isn't it?"

"That's right," Mahler conceded.

"To go all these years—and find *you*. Talk about wild improbabilities! "

Mahler ignored him, declining to take up the challenge. He had found it to be good practice never to let a captured jumper get the upper hand in conversation. His standard procedure was firmly to explain to the jumper just why it was imperative for him to be sent to the Moon, and then to summon the guards as quickly as possible.

"You say this is a two-way time rig?" Mahler asked, holding up the flimsy-looking piece of equipment.

"That's right," the other agreed. "It works both ways. If you pressed the button you'd go straight back to the year two thousand, three hundred and sixty, or thereabouts."

"Did you build it?"

"Me? No, hardly," said the jumper. "I found it. It's a long story and I don't have time to tell it now. In fact, if I tried to tell it I'd only make things ten times worse than they are. No. Let's get this over with as quickly as we can, shall we? I know I don't stand much of a chance with you, and I'd just as soon make it quick."

"You know, of course, that this is a world without disease—" Mahler began sonorously.

"And that you think I'm carrying enough germs of different sorts to wipe out the whole world. And therefore you have to be absolutely inflexible with me. All right. I won't try to argue with you. Which way is the Moon?"

Absolutely inflexible. The phrase Mahler had used so many times, the phrase that summed him up so neatly! He chuckled to himself. Some of the younger technicians must have tipped off the jumper about the usual procedure, and the jumper had resigned himself to going peacefully, without bothering to plead. It was just as well.

Absolutely inflexible.

Yes, Mahler thought, the words fitted him well. He was becoming a stereotype in the Bureau. Perhaps he was the only Bureau Chief who had never relented, and let a jumper go. Probably all of the others, bowed under the weight of hordes of curious men flooding in from the past, had finally cracked and taken the risk.

But not Mahler—not Absolutely Inflexible Mahler. He took pride in the deep responsibility that rode on his shoulders, and had no intention of evading a sacred trust. His job was to find the jumpers and get them off Earth as quickly and as efficiently as possible. Every single one. It was a task that required relentless inflexibility.

"This makes my job much easier," Mahler said. "I'm glad I won't have to convince you that I am simply doing my duty."

"Not at all," the other said. "I understand. I won't even waste my breath. The task you must carry out is understandable, and I cannot hope to make you change your mind." He turned to the guards. "I'm ready. Take me away."

Mahler gestured to them, and they led the jumper away. Amazed, Mahler watched the retreating figure, studying him until he could no longer be seen.

If they were all like that, Mahler thought. *I could have gotten to like that one. He was a sensible man—one of the few. He knew he was beaten, and he didn't try to argue in the face of absolute necessity. It's too bad he had to go. He's the kind of man I'd like to find more often these days. But I mustn't feel sympathy. That would be unwise.*

100

Mahler had succeeded as an administrator only because he had managed to suppress any sympathy for the unfortunates he had been compelled to condemn. Had there been any other place to send them—back to their own time, preferably—he would have been the first to urge abolition of the Moon prison. But, with only one course of action open to him, he performed his job efficiently and automatically.

He picked up the jumper's time rig and examined it. A two-way rig would be the solution, of course. As soon as the jumper arrived, a new and better policy would be in force, turning him around and sending him back. They'd get the idea quickly enough. Mahler found himself wishing it could be so; he often wondered what the jumpers stranded on the Moon must think of him.

A two-way rig would change the world so completely that its implications would be staggering. With men able to move at will backward and forward in time the past, present, and future would blend into one broad and shining highway. It was impossible to conceive of the world as it might be, with free passage in either direction.

But even as Mahler fondled the confiscated time rig he realized that something was wrong. In the six centuries since the attainment of time travel, no one had yet developed a known two-way rig. And an unknown rig was pretty well ruled out. There were no documented reports of visitors from the future and presumably, if such a rig existed, such visitors would have been as numerous as were the jumpers from the past.

So the young man had been lying, Mahler thought with regret. The two-way rig was an utter impossibility. The youth had merely been playing a game with his captors. There *couldn't* be a two-way rig, because the past had never been in any way influenced by the future.

Mahler examined the rig. There were two dials on it— the conventional forward dial and another indicating backward travel. Whoever had prepared the incredible hoax had gone to considerable trouble to document it. *Why?*

Could it be that the jumper had been telling the truth? Mahler wished that he could somehow test the rig immediately. There was always the one slim chance that it might actually work, and that he would no longer have to be a rigid dispenser of justice. Absolutely Inflexible Mahler!

He looked at it. As a time machine, it was fairly crude. It made use of the standard distorter pattern, but the dial was the clumsy wide-range 24th-Century one. The vernier system, Mahler reflected, had not been introduced until the 25th Century.

Mahler peered closer to read the instruction label. PLACE LEFT HAND HERE, it said. He studied it carefully. The ghost of a thought wandered into his mind. He pushed it aside in horror, but it recurred. It would be so simple. What if he should—

No.

But—

PLACE LEFT HAND HERE.

He reached out tentatively with his left hand.

Be careful now. No sense in being reckless—

PLACE LEFT HAND HERE.

PRESS DIAL.

He placed his left hand lightly on the indicated place. There was a little crackle of electricity. He let go, quickly, and started to replace the time rig when the desk abruptly faded out from under him.

The air was foul and grimy. Mahler wondered what had happened to the Conditioner. Then he looked around.

Huge, grotesque, ugly buildings blocked out most of the sky. There were dark oppressive clouds of smoke overhead, and the harsh screech of an industrial society assailed his ears.

He was in the middle of an immense city, and streams of people were rushing past him at a furious pace. They were all small, stunted creatures, their faces harried and neurotic. They all had the same despairing, frightened look. It was an expression Mahler had seen many times on the faces of jumpers escaping from an unendurable nightmare world to a more congenial future.

He stared down at the time rig clutched in his hand, and knew what had happened. The two-way rig!

It meant the end of the Moon prisons. It meant a complete revolution in civilization. But he had no desire to remain in so oppressive and horrible an age a minute longer than was necessary. He reached down to activate the time rig.

Abruptly someone jolted him from behind and the current of the crowd swept him along. He was struggling desperately to regain control over himself when a hand reached out and gripped the back of his neck.

"Got a card, Hump?" a harsh voice demanded.

He whirled to face an ugly, squinting-eyed man in a dull-brown uniform.

"Did you hear what I said? Where's your card, Hump? Talk up or you get Spotted."

Mahler twisted out of the man's grasp and started to jostle his way quickly through the crowd, desiring nothing more than an opportunity to set the time rig and get out of this disease-ridden, squalid era forever. As he shoved people out of his way they shouted angrily and tried to trip him, raining blows on his back and shoulders.

"There's a Hump! " someone called. "Spot him! "

The cry became a roar. "Spot him! Spot him! Spot him! "

He turned left and went pounding down a side street, and now it was a full-fledged mob that dashed after him, shouting in savage fury.

"Send for the Crimers!" a deep voice boomed. "They'll Spot him!"

A running man caught up to him and in sheer desperation Mahler swung about and let fly with his fists. He heard a dull grunt of pain, but he did not pause in his headlong flight. The unaccustomed exercise was tiring him rapidly.

An open door beckoned, and he hurried swiftly toward it.

An instant later he was inside a small furniture shop and a salesman was advancing toward him. "Can I help you, sir? The latest models, right here."

"Just leave me alone," Mahler panted, squinting at the time rig.

The salesman stared uncomprehendingly as Mahler fumbled with the little dial.

There was no vernier. He'd have to chance it and hope to hit the right year. The salesman suddenly screamed and came to life—for reasons Mahler would never understand.

Mahler ignored him and punched the stud viciously.

It was wonderful to step back into the serenity of 28th-Century Appalachia. It was small wonder so many time jumpers came to so peaceful an age, Mahler reflected, as he waited for his overworked heart to calm down. Almost anything would be preferable to *back there*.

He looked up and down the quiet street, seeking a Convenience where he could repair the scratches and bruises he had acquired during his brief stay in the past. They would scarcely be able to recognize him at the bureau in his present battered condition, with one eye nearly closed, and a great livid welt on his cheek.

He sighted one at last and started down the street, only to be brought up short by the sound of a familiar soft mechanical whining. He looked around to see one of the low-running mechanical tracers of the bureau purring up the street toward him. It was closely followed by two bureau guards, clad in their protective casings.

Of course! He had arrived from the past, and the detectors had recorded his arrival, just as they would have pinpointed any time traveler. They never missed.

He turned, and walked toward the guards. He failed to recognize them, but this did not surprise him. The bureau was a vast and wide-ranging organization, and he knew only a handful of the many guards who customarily accompanied the tracers. It was a pleasant relief to see the tracer. The use of tracers had been instituted during his administration, and he was absolutely sure now that he hadn't returned too early along the time stream.

"Good to see you," he called to the approaching guards. "I had a little accident in the office."

They ignored him, and began methodically to unpack a spacesuit from the storage trunk of the mechanical tracer.

"Never mind talking," one said. "Get into this."

He paled. "But I'm no jumper," he protested. "Hold on a moment, fellows. This is all a terrible mistake. I'm Mahler—head of the bureau. *Your boss.*"

"Don't play games with us, chum," the taller guard said, while the other forced the spacesuit down over Mahler's shoulders. To his horror, Mahler saw that they did not recognize him at all.

"Suppose you just come peacefully and let the chief explain everything to you, without any trouble," the short guard said.

"But I *am* the chief," Mahler protested. "I was examining a two-way time rig in my office and accidentally sent myself back to the past. Take this thing off me and I'll show you my identification card. That should convince you."

"Look, chum, we don't want to be convinced of anything. Tell it to the chief, if you like. Now, are you coming —or do we bring you?"

There was no point, Mahler decided, in trying to prove his identity to the clean-faced young medic who examined him at the bureau office. To insist on an immediate identification would only add more complications. No. It would be far better to wait until he reached the office of the chief.

He knew now what had happened. Apparently he had landed somewhere in his own future, shortly after his own death. Someone else had taken over the bureau, and he, Mahler had been forgotten. He suddenly realized with a little shock that at that very moment his ashes were probably reposing in an urn at the Appalachia Crematorium.

When he got to the chief of the bureau, he would simply and calmly explain exactly what had happened and ask for permission to go back ten or twenty or thirty years to the time in which he belonged. Once there, he could turn the two-way rig over to the proper authorities and resume his life from his point of departure. When that happened, the jumpers would no longer be sent to the Moon, and there would be no further need for Inflexible Mahler.

But, he suddenly realized, if he'd already done that why was there still a clearance bureau? An uneasy fear began to grow in him.

"Hurry up and finish that report," Mahler told the medic.

"I don't know what the rush is," the medic complained. "Unless you like it on the Moon."

"Don't worry about me," Mahler said confidently. "If I told you who I am, you'd think twice about—"

"Is this thing your time rig?" the medic asked unexpectedly.

"Not really. I mean—yes, yes it is," Mahler said. "And be careful with it. It's the world's only two-way rig."

"Really, now! " said the medic. "Two ways, eh?"

"Yes. And if you'll take me to your chief—"

"Just a minute. I'd like to show this to the head medic."

In a few moments the medic returned. "All right, we'll go to the chief now. I'd advise you not to bother arguing with him. You can't win. You should have stayed in your own age."

Two guards appeared and jostled Mahler down the familiar corridor to the brightly lit little office where he had spent eight years of his life. Eight years on the other side of the fence!

As he approached the room that had once been his office, he carefully planned what he would say to his successor. He would explain the accident first, of course. Then he would establish his identity beyond any possibility of doubt and request permission to use the two-way rig to return to his own time. The chief would probably be belligerent at first. But he'd quickly enough become curious, and finally amused at the chain of events that had ensnarled Mahler.

And, of course, he would make amends, after they had exchanged anecdotes about the job they both held at the same time across a wide gap of years. Mahler vowed that he would never again touch a time machine, once he got back. He would let others undertake the huge job of transmitting the jumpers back to their own eras.

He moved forward and broke the photoelectric beam. The door to the bureau chief's office slid open. Behind the desk sat a tall, powerfully built man with hard gray eyes.

Me!

Through the dim plate of the spacesuit into which he had been stuffed, Mahler stared in stunned horror at the man behind the desk. It was impossible for him to doubt that he was gazing at Inflexible Mahler, the man who had sent four thousand men to the Moon, without exception, in the unbending pursuit of his duty.

And if he's Mahler—

Who am I?

Suddenly Mahler saw the insane circle complete. He recalled the jumper, the firm, deep-voiced, unafraid time jumper who had arrived claiming to have a two-way rig and who had marched off to the Moon without arguing. Now Mahler knew who that strange jumper was.

But how did the cycle start? Where had the two-way rig come from in the first place? He had gone to the past to bring it to the present to take it to the past to—

His head swam. There was no way out. He looked at the man behind the desk and began to walk slowly toward him, feeling a wall of circumstance growing up around him, while in frustration he tried impotently to beat his way out.

It was utterly pointless to argue. Not with Absolutely Inflexible Mahler. It would just be a waste of breath. The wheel had come full circle, and he was as good as on the Moon already. He looked at the man behind the desk with a new, strange light in his eyes.

"I never dreamed I'd find you here," the jumper said. The transmitter of the spacesuit brought the jumper's voice over deeply and resonantly.

HIS BROTHER'S WEEPER

The Deserializing Room at Cincinnati Spaceport was, Peter Martlett thought, a little on the bleak side. It was no more than twenty feet square, illuminated by a single hooded fluorobulb, and was bare of all ornament. In the center of the floorspace stood the awesome bulk of the Henderson Deserializer. Two white-smocked technicians flanked it, staring eagerly at Martlett, who had just entered. Behind him sounded the noisy hum of the waiting room he had quitted. There was a lot of deserializing going on today.

"Mr. Martlett?"

Martlett nodded tensely. He was more than a little leery of submitting himself to the Deserializer, especially after what had happened to his brother Michael. But the travel-agency people had assured him that that had been a fluke, one-in-a-million, one-in-a-billion—

"May we have your passport?" said the thinner and more efficient looking of the two technicians. Martlett surrendered it, along with his accident claim waiver, his identification ticket, his departure permit, and the pre-stamped entrance visa that would allow him to visit Marathon where his brother had gone to a hideous death the month before.

Heads almost touching, the pair of them riffled quickly through Martlett's papers, nodded in agreement, and gestured for him to take a seat in the Deserializer. One of the technicians produced a dark enameled square box a foot on each side and proceeded to attach Martlett's documents to it with stickons. Moistening his lips, Martlett watched. In a very few minutes, he knew, he himself would be inside the box.

The other deserializing technician strapped Martlett firmly into the Deserializer and lowered a metal cone over his head. In a soothing voice he said, "Of course you understand the approximate nature of the Deserializer, sir—"

"Yes, I—"

Ignoring the outburst, the technician continued what was obviously a memorized speech delivered before each departure. "The Henderson Deserializer makes possible instantaneous traffic between stars. The deserializing field induces distortion of the four coordinate axes of your worldline, removing you temporarily from contact with the temporal axis and—for convenience in storage—somewhat compressing you along the three spatial axes."

"You mean I'll be put in that little box?"

"Exactly, sir. You and your luggage will enter this container and you will be placed aboard a spaceship bound for the planet of your destination. Ah—Marathon, I believe. Although the journey to Marathon requires two hundred eighty-three objective years, for you it will be a matter of seconds—since, of course, on your arrival you will enter another deserializing field that will restore you to your temporal axis at a point only seconds after you had left it on Earth!"

"In short," the other technician chimed in, "you enter a box here, are shipped to Marathon, and are unpacked there—total elapsed time, ten seconds. If you choose to return to Earth immediately on arrival, you could do that. If you felt like it, you could make nearly thirty round trips a minute, eighteen hundred an hour—"

"If I could afford it," Martlett said dryly. The round trip

110

fare was nine hundred units, and it was making a considerable dent in his savings. But, of course, the Colonial Government of Marathon had asked him to make the trip, to settle his brother's unfinished affairs. And the shock of Michael's tragic death had been such that he had agreed at once to make the trip.

"Heh heh," chuckled the technician. "To be sure, eighteen hundred round trips *would* be on the costly side! Heh heh heh—"

The two technicians chuckled harmoniously, all the while bustling round Martlett and making adjustments in the complex network of dials and levers that hemmed him in on all sides. He was just beginning to get annoyed at all the laughter when—

Whick!

—he found himself lying on a plush, well-padded couch in a room walled mostly with curving glass. The sun was in his eyes—bluish-purple sunlight. Green-tinted clouds drifted lazily in the auburn sky. Two smiling technicians in sheen-gray coveralls were nodding at him in smug satisfaction.

"Welcome to Marathon, Mr. Martlett."

Martlett licked his lips. "I'm here?"

"You are. Transshipped from Cincinnati Spaceport, Earth, aboard the good ship *Venus*. Today is the 11th of April, 2209, Galactic Standard Time."

"The same day I left Earth!"

"Of course, Mr. Martlett, of course! The Henderson Deserializer—"

"Yes, yes, I know," Martlett interjected hastily, forestalling yet another rendition of the Information for Travelers Speech. "I fully understand the process." He looked around. "I'm here on request of your Secretary for Internal Affairs, Mr. Jansen. It's about my brother—"

The word was ill-chosen. It triggered a strong reaction in

111

the two deserializer men. They coughed and reddened and glanced obliquely over Martlett's head as if they were very embarrassed. Martlett pressed on undisturbed. "My brother Michael, who was a colonist here until his unfortunate death in a Deserializer accident last month. Do you know where I can find the secre—"

"He's waiting outside to see you," said the short technician with the swerving nose.

"And we wish to assure you that this office has been cleared of all responsibility in the matter of your brother's —ah—disappearance," put in the tall one with the unconvincing yellow toupee.

Martlett stared at them sourly. "I'm not here to press charges," he said. "Just to settle my late brother's affairs."

He rose, feeling a bit stiff around the knees. Not surprising, he thought, considering he had just spent two hundred eighty-three objective years in an enameled box one foot square. Gathering up his papers, he stepped out into the antechamber, discovering as he walked that Marathon's gravity was only about two-thirds that of Earth. It was all he could do to keep himself from skipping. Skipping, he thought, would hardly look decorous on a man whose beloved brother had gone to an untimely death only five Galactic Standard Weeks before.

The Marathonian Secretary for Internal Affairs introduced himself as Octavian Jansen, a fact Martlett already knew. He was a tall, stoop-shouldered man of dignified appearance and middle age. His office, he said, was within walking distance of the Arrivals Center, and so they walked there. Martlett enjoyed the springy sensation of walking at two-thirds grav. He threw his head back, breathing in the clean, fresh air. Overhead, colorful birds wheeled and screeched playfully. Swaying palmoid trees lined the streets. Marathon, Michael had often written to him, was nothing more or less than a paradise. Fertile soil, extravagantly satisfactory climate, no native carnivorous

112

life forms bigger than caninoids and felinoids, and the women!

Yes, the women! Michael had always had a good eye for the women, Martlett reflected.

Jansen's office was handsomely furnished. A brace of hunting trophies loomed on one wall, great lowering massive purple-skinned trihorned heads: Marathon's largest life form, the ponderous, herbivorous, harmless hippopotamoids. Sleek freeform chairs faced the freeform onyx-topped desk. Martlett pulled one up.

Jansen said, "May I remark that you look astonishingly like your late brother, Mr. Martlett?"

"Many people thought we were twins."

"You are the older brother?"

"By three years. I'm 30. Michael is—was—27."

For a moment Jansen's eyes dropped respectfully. "Your brother was very popular here, Mr. Martlett. From the day he joined our colony two years ago, he was a leader of the community. And I needn't tell you how much we admired his music! Only next month our local symphony orchestra was to have presented an all-Martlett concert: the Second Symphony, the Theremin Concerto, and a piece for strings and synthesizer called simply *Amor*."

Martlett nodded. Michael's success here was part of an old story. Michael, no more handsome than he, no taller and no more muscular, had always been the gregarious brother, surrounded by admirers and adored by women. While he, Peter, the older brother and presumably the wiser, was instead regarded as a sort of bumbling foster uncle, not too clever, who needed help in all he undertook. And so it had gone. In a world where a serious composer stood no chance at all against the symphonic computers, Michael had won indellible musical fame at the age of twenty-three. Two years later, he had pocketed a fat fellowship and departed for the pleasant world of Marathon to continue his composing, far from the jarring dissonances of Terran life.

And now, at twenty-seven, he was dead. The older brother, shy, uncertain Peter, had the task of gathering together the reins Michael had abruptly dropped, collecting his belongings, settling his debts.

"Has the concert been cancelled?" Martlett asked.

"Oh, no," Jansen said. "It's being done as a memorial. Your brother was to have conducted himself, but we've hired someone else. It's to be given on the fifteenth of May. I do hope you'll attend."

"Sorry," Martlett said brusquely. "I wasn't planning to stay on Marathon more than a week or two—just long enough to do whatever needs to be done about Michael's affairs. By the middle of May I'll be back on Earth, I'm afraid."

"As you wish, of course." Jansen shrugged mournfully. "I've taken the liberty of assembling a portfolio of bills that your brother left unpaid at the time of his death."

Martlett took the bulky folder from him and opened it. The uppermost bill was from the Marathon Deserialized Instantaneous Transportation Corporation: 110 units charged for a journey from Marathon to the neighboring world of Thermopylae, ten units down and six months to pay.

"I hardly think *this* bill needs to be paid," Martlett said, nudging it across the desk to Jansen.

The secretary looked at it, flushed, and said quickly, "Ah —of course not—an error, Mr. Martlett—"

An error indeed, Martlett thought. That journey had never been completed. Michael had entered the De-serializer on Marathon, and ostensibly was to have arrived on Thermopylae, ninety million miles away, almost at once. But the Deserializer box had been empty when it reached Thermopylae. Somewhere in mid-journey Michael had disappeared, his compressed and deserialized body shunted off irrevocably into some parellel continuum, into that dark bourn from which no traveler returns.

The law in such cases—they were one-in-a-billion occurrences—was plain. The missing party was to be considered legally dead. No one had ever returned who had disappeared in mid-jaunt via Deserializer.

Martlett thumbed through the rest of the bills. They were small ones, but there were plenty of them—a heavy liquor tab, five florists' bills, an invoice from a men's clothier and a larger one from a woman's outfitter, and so on. Evidently Michael had not lost his old touch with the women, Martlett thought.

The total, he computed roughly, was in the vicinity of three thousand units. He could afford the outlay; the royalties from Michael's music, whose performance rights he had automatically inherited, would reimburse him soon enough.

"Very well," Martlett said. "I'll take care of all these matters right away. Now, if there are any other—"

"Yes," Jansen said gravely. "I believe you should know there was a woman. A—well—ah—your brother's fiancée."

"His *what*? Why, Michael used to swear day and night he'd never let himself get trapped into marrying!"

"Be that as it may, this woman claims he made a definite promise to her. I think you ought to pay a call on her—ah —in the interests of good form, you know."

Her name was Sondra Bullard. Martlett went to visit her that evening, after he had finished installing himself in his brother's palmoid-ringed fourteen-room villa. She lived half a continent away—Marathon was somewhat on the sprawling side—and Martlett found it necessary to charter an aircab to get there.

Sondra Bullard's dwelling was modest compared to Michael's—a ranch-type affair that rambled over a few

115

acres of grassy meadow at the foot of a handsome plunging waterfall. A gleaming jetcar jutted from the open garage. Martlett wondered in passing if Michael had bought her these things. He had always been extravagant.

Feeling a little uneasy, Martlett strode up the flagstoned walk and stepped into the green scanner field that glowed round the door. A chime sounded within, calling Miss Bullard's attention to the fact that she had a visitor; a moment went by, and then a piercing shriek was distinctly audible.

Martlett felt perspiration begin to bead his forehead. Before he could give way completely to alarm and turn to run, the front door opened and Miss Sondra Bullard peered out at him. She was dressed unsurprisingly in black, and her face was astonishingly pale. She was also, Martlett noted, quite lovely. Michael's taste had always been impeccable.

"You're—Michael's—*brother?*"

"That's right. Peter Martlett. I called earlier, you remember."

"Yes. Won't you come in?" She spoke mechanically, chopping each word off into an individual sentence.

Once he was inside she said, "You—look very much like your brother, you know."

"So I've been told."

"I was frightened when I saw your image in the scanner field." She laughed in self-deprecation. "I guess I thought it was Michael at the door. Silly of me, but you two *did* look so much alike. Were you twins?"

"I was three years the elder."

"Oh."

After a few lame moments of silence the girl said, "Drink?"

"Yes, please. Something mild."

She dialed a filtered rum for him and a stiff highball for herself. While he sipped, Martlett surreptitiously looked around. A lot of cash had been tossed into these furnishings, and it seemed to him he recognized his brother's fine hand—and money—in the decorating scheme. He felt a momentary current of anger; this girl, he thought, had been *milking* Michael!

Oh, no, came the immediate inner denial. Michael had been nobody's fool. He wasn't susceptible to gold-digging.

Hesitantly Martlett said, "Secretary Jansen was telling me you knew Michael quite well."

"We were engaged," she said immediately.

Since he had been warned, Martlett was able to avoid the double take. "Odd, Michael never wrote to me about it. Had you known him long?"

"Six months. We became engaged nine weeks ago. We were supposed to be married the first week in June." Her lower lip trembled a bit. "And then—I got the phone call —they told me—"

A tear rolled down her lovely cheek, and she dabbed at it. Martlett felt uncomfortable. Why, this was almost like paying a call on a new widow! She was in mourning and all.

He said, "I know how you must feel, Miss—ah—Miss Bullard. Michael was a wonderful person—so dynamic, so full of life—"

"And now he's *gone*!" she wailed. "Poof! Vanished off into some other continuum, they told me! Living on some horrible world without air somewhere, maybe!"

"They say it's a quick and painless way to die," Martlett ventured. The words did not soothe her.

The single tear became a torrent; her well-equipped bosom heaved with convulsive sobs. Watching her, Martlett's lips twitched in dismay. Open display of emotion had always been a tribulation for him to witness. He himself felt grief at his brother's passing, certainly, but he had never given way to—to this—

But the sobbing became contagious. "I loved him," she

moaned. "And he's gone! Gone!" She groped out blindly, fumbled her way onto his shoulder, and ler her emotions go. Martlett felt his eyes growing misty at the thought of this girl who had built her whole life around his undeniably remarkable brother, and who now faced nothing but emptiness. Before he knew it, he was crying too.

They sobbed on each other's shoulders for a few moments; then, the fit passing, they straightened up and looked at each other. Her gray eyes were red-rimmed.

"You're so much like him," she murmured. "So tall, so handsome, so—*understanding*."

He felt his face reddening, and nervously moistened his lips. The grief had seemed to fade from her features, and now some other emotion took its place—an emotion Martlett, in thirty years of bachelorhood, had come to recognize with an expert's skill.

Disengaging himself from her, he rose. "I'll have to leave you now, Miss Bullard. It's been a difficult day for me, you understand. But I'll try to see you again before I return to Earth. We've both lost someone very dear to us. Good night, Miss Bullard."

"Why don't you call me Sondra."

He smiled uneasily. "Good night—Sondra."

"Good night, Peter."

Martlett slept that night in his brother's bed, which was a palatial triple-size monstrosity with a pink velvet canopy and a soothing built-in tranquilophone. Martlett found the murmuring wordless sounds of the tranquilophone distracting, but there was no way to shut the thing off, and finally he fell asleep despite it. He dreamed odd dreams and woke feeling unrefreshed in the morning.

Michael's robot butler had prepared a meal for him, Martlett discovered. He wondered whether the robot was aware that the person in the house was *not* his master. Probably not; so far as the robot was concerned, the

118

human of the house *looked* like Mr. Martlett, answered to the name, and therefore *was* Mr. Martlett. That he was the wrong Mr. Martlett did not seem to matter. Robot brains were not geared to such niceties.

Martlett ate thoughtfully, taking his meal on the veranda overlooking Michael's private lake. Sweet-smelling morning breezes drifted toward him. Michael had written that "it is springtime all the year round on Marathon," and he had been telling the truth. Although this was the first time Martlett had visited one of the colony worlds, or indeed had left Earth for any reason at all, he found it hard to imagine a planet more lovely than this one. It would almost be a pity, once he had concluded his business here, to have to return to crowded, untidy Earth once again and go back to the weary business of constructing mindless video jingles.

Better, he thought, to stay here in this eternal springtime—

No.

He shut off the thought promptly. Whatever he did, he did *not* intend to become a colonist on Marathon. His place was on Earth. Let escapists like Michael flee to this utopian planet; doubtless laziness and indolence triumphed here, and in a few short generations decadence would be rampant.

The butler came slithering out on the veranda, rolling noiselessly on its treads. "There is a phone call for you, master."

"For me? Can I take it out here?"

The robot registered confusion for an instant. "Surely you know that there is no pickup connection out here, Mr. Martlett?"

"Of course. Silly of me to forget that!"

He followed the robot inside and, tugging his dressing gown tight around himself, entered the camera field of the vidphone. There was a woman's face on the screen—a

119

rather attractive face, Martlett observed, blue-eyed and framed in lustrous blonde hair.

"Good morning," he said, in a flat noncommittal voice.

"Oh—you look so much like him! "

"Yes. We almost looked like twins," Martlett said, a trifle edgily. "But I was three years his elder."

"You must be Peter, then. He told me so much about you! "

"Did he? How kind of him. May I ask who it is that I am—"

"Didn't he send you my photo?"

Martlett frowned. "Not that I recall—and I'm sure that I *would* recall, if he had. I'm afraid he didn't."

"Strange," the girl said. "He said he was mailing you a tridim of me. I'm Joanne Hastings."

"Pleased to meet you, Miss Hastings," Martlett said blankly, wondering who Joanne Hastings might be.

She furrowed her forehead prettily. "I said, *Joanne Hastings*. You mean Michael didn't tell you *that* either? Obviously he didn't, because you don't seem to recognize my name at all."

An ominous premonition clogged Martlett's throat. In a hushed voice he said, "I'm afraid Michael didn't tell me anything about you, Miss Hastings."

"Call me Joanne. I am—was—Michael's fiancée. We were going to be married in June, you see."

"Oh. Oh, yes. Yes, I see, Miss Hastings. You and he— were going to get married—in June—"

Martlett closed his eyes briefly, and the image of Sondra Bullard wandered unbidden across the inside of his eyelids. Sondra was a brunette. This girl was a blonde. And Michael had been engaged to both of them.

Suddenly Martlett understood many things he had not been cognizant of before. He realized why Michael had abruptly taken that ill-fated journey to Thermopylae. That it had ended tragically was unfortunate, Martlett reflected

—but the Deserializer accident *had* saved Michael from a devilishly nasty dilemma, anyway. Both Joanne and Sondra seemed the predatory kind. Had Michael reached Thermopylae safely, they no doubt would have pursued him there —and from there to Mycenae, and from Mycenae to Thebes, and from there to any other world to which he might flee. Poor Michael! Some of Martlett's grief abated. Had Michael lived, he would never have escaped the clutches of the two females to whom he had so inadvisedly pledged his troth.

With tenderness Martlett said, "I understand, Miss Hastings. His death must have been a dreadful blow to you. As it was to all of us, of course; I loved my brother dearly."

Before he had finished his conversation with Joanne Hastings, he found himself accepting a dinner invitation to her ranch eight hundred miles southward, for the next night. She wanted to talk to him about Michael, and it would have been churlish of him to refuse. He tactfully resolved not to mention to her the matter of Michael's *other* fiancée who called in midmorning, while Martlett was busily wading through the backlog of Michael's unpaid bills and scribbling checks on the veranda. He had dealt with about half of them already; the expenditure so far had been nearly twenty-five hundred units. His rough estimate of three thousand altogether had clearly been inaccurate. But Michael's symphonies would bring royalties forever, Martlett told himself consolingly, as he crossed the veranda and headed for the nearest vidphone at the robot's beck.

Sondra was inconsolably lonely, she sobbed to him, and wanted him to visit her for lunch that day. "You reminded me so much of Michael," she confided. "When you were with me last night I almost felt as though *he* were here!"

Obligingly, Martlett chartered a jetcar once again and flew to her villa for lunch. The visit dragged on until evening, and when Marathon's single big golden moon had spiraled into the sky she insisted he stay for dinner as well. He began to sense that getting Michael's bills paid might take longer than he had expected, at this rate.

He succeeded in disentangling himself by midevening, and flew home deep in brooding thought. The girl seemed perfectly willing to accept him as a substitute for Michael. Most remarkable, he thought. True, there was a physical resemblance so great as to be uncanny, considering the difference in their ages, but as far as personality went they were vastly different. Michael had been flamboyant, witty, spectacular and even a trifle sensational; his older brother tended more toward introspection and sobriety, and most of Michael's women had accordingly shown little interest in Peter's existence. But things seemed to be different with Sondra Bullard, Martlett reflected.

And with Joanne Hastings as well, he discovered the following night, when he kept his dinner engagement with her. He had spent the day in conference with a few of Michael's creditors, people who had neglected to present bills to Secretary Jansen and who now hastened to offer them to Peter.

There was a matter of four hundred units for piano repairs, and three hundred more for music paper. A liquor and wine merchant had sold Michael five magnums of champagne, imported from Earth, fifty units apiece. And so on and so on. The tab was mounting; Martlett estimated he had paid out nearly five thousand units to the creditors of his late brother in these two days, and he was a long way from finished. He wondered how long it would be before Michael's estate earned back five thousand units in royalties, not to mention the nine hundred more it had cost him to come out here.

He was in a morbid frame of mind when he reached Joanne Hastings' ranch, but she soon dispelled his mood. She greeted him dressed in a gay and skimpy plasti-spray

122

outfit that belied her recent loss, and there were cocktails waiting on a tray in the sunken living room.

"You *are* so much like Michael," she told him. "You have the same dark eyes, the same untidy hair, the same way of smiling—"

"Thank you," Martlett said uncertainly. He realized such a situation, but he admitted bleakly to himself that he was not Michael, no matter what these strange women seemed to think.

"It's odd Michael didn't tell you he was planning to marry," she said.

"He never confided much in me," Martlett replied. "Not about such matters, anyway."

"June eighth, it would have been." She sighed. "Well, now it's never to be. Mrs. Michael Martlett—you know, I used to spend hours practising signing my name that way! But—well—"

A lump was beginning to form in Martlett's throat. She seemed so poised, so resigned now to Michael's being dead, and yet behind the outward mask he could plainly see how deeply she felt her loss. He said, "I wish there were something I could do for you, Miss Hastings—"

"Joanne."

"Joanne. But I can't bring Michael back, can I?"

"No," she agreed, after a moment's solemn thought. "No, you can't. All that talent lost in a moment! What a waste!"

"Yes," he said sadly. "What a waste."

She moved a bit closer to him on the couch, and he decided it would be impolite to edge away. She said, "You're *so* much like Michael, dear."

Dear? he wondered. What next?

He said, "You're upset, Miss—Joanne. Let me pour you another drink."

"Yes, do." She moved closer still. "And pour one for yourself."

Somehow it was not at all surprising when he discovered she had her arms around him, and was maneuvering toward him in a way that left him no alternative but to kiss her.

In the next few days, Martlett discerned a clear pattern taking shape, and it frightened him. Not a day went by without a call from one or both of Michael's fiancées, inviting him for dinner. And he was too innately polite to be able to decline their offers.

But, as he spent his days paying Michael's bills (the figure had mounted to seven thousand five hundred units now, and still the creditors arrived in fresh troops) and his evenings sipping cocktails with Michael's betrotheds, he realized what was happening. Both girls—each unaware of the other's presence in the scheme of things—had evidently resolved that if they could not have Michael, they very well were going to have Michael's brother. Martlett was an acceptable substitute to them. Each was spinning a web for him, hoping to trap him into the matrimony he had successfully avoided for thirty consecutive years.

The thought frightened him.

He had come to Marathon to bury Michael, not to inherit his fiancées. It had been his plan to settle Michael's financial affairs, not his romantic ones. He fondly expected to return to Earth in a week or two, still a single man. But yet these girls seemed to be pinning their hopes on snaring him. With each passing day they took less care to hide their true intent.

"Do you still insist on going back to Earth when you've tidied up Michael's bills?" Sondra wanted to know.

"My leave was only for two weeks. I—"

"You could tell your employers you weren't coming back. There must be some advertising agency you could work for on Marathon. And we could live in Michael's villa—"

"We?"

124

She reddened. "Sorry, darling. Slip of the tongue. Have another martini, Peter. This Denebian vermouth is delightful."

Eight hours later he was a thousand miles away, consuming cognac in Joanne Hastings' marbled atrium. He had put off Sondra's increasingly more urgent proposals with vague delayers and demurs, but now Joanne was saying, "Peter, dear, you aren't *really* going back to Earth, are you?"

"As soon as I've finished what I came here to do," he said as stolidly as he could considering the amount of alcohol he had ingested that day.

"Which was?"

"To tidy up the loose ends of Michael's fabric of existence, so to speak," he said.

Her delicate eyebrows lifted a fraction of a millimeter. "But—*I'm* one of Michael's loose ends, darling! "

Martlett sighed wearily. "Let's not talk about it now, Joanne. Play that tape of Michael's symphony, would you?"

By midday of his ninth day on Marathon, Peter Martlett had at last concluded the job of settling the late Michael Martlett's affairs. All the bills were paid, including three-thousand-unit mortgage payment on Michael's villa; the total damage had been just under fourteen thousand units, which had wiped out Martlett's savings entirely. Michael's banker had given him the comforting news that he could expect an income of from ten to fifteen thousand units annually from Michael's musical compositions; the fame of a composer always increased immediately after his death, and in Michael's case the tragic circumstance was sure to create a Galaxywide demand for his works.

There was merely the matter of Michael's fiancées to be settled before he left.

Martlett's ethical soul recoiled at the thought of ducking out and popping back to Earth via the Deserializer without even a good-by, but he knew that was the only possible solution. If he risked calling either or both of them that he was leaving, he could be sure they would artfully ply their wiles and see to it that he remained on Marathon a while longer.

Women, he thought sourly. They bait their hooks with emotion and watch us wriggle when we're caught.

If he spoke to them, they would surely be able to make him stay. And if he stayed, the question of matrimony would inevitably come up. And—the premise followed in rigorous logical sequence—one or the other of the girls would suffer disappointment, while he himself would undergo the equally grave loss of his freedom.

He saw clearly why Michael had decided to bolt to Thermopylae. Lucky Michael had vanished en route, though! He had escaped both forever. And, as had happened so often in the past, it was Big Brother who had to stay around to face the music.

He considered the situation a while. The gentlemanly thing to do—well, there *was* no gentlemanly thing to do. He had both of his brother's women on his hands, and all he could do under the circumstances was run, and fast. Better to jilt both than one, he thought; that way neither would learn that there had been a rival for her affections all along.

After due consideration he phoned Secretary Jansen and announced, "I'm finished with the job. Every debt of Michael's has been paid and I've arranged for the disposition of his personal belongings."

"Glad to hear that. We're pleased you could make the trip, and I hope you enjoyed your stay on Marathon."

"Certainly," Martlett replied. "A wonderful planet. But my work on Earth awaits me. How soon can I have accommodations on the outward journey?"

"You're in luck—a ship leaves for Earth at midnight.

You can show up any time, as late as eleven, to be deserialized and placed on board."

"I'll be there," Martlett said.

He broke the contact, feeling an abiding sense of guilt. *So I'm a cad, he thought. So what? I didn't ask them to fall in love with me. They aren't in love with me, anyway. Just with Michael's image.*

He was half finished with the task of packing his meager belongings when the phone chime sounded. Activating the controls, he was dismayed to see the blonde tresses of Joanne Hastings in three dimensions and natural color.

"Peter—I hear you're leaving!"

"Where did you get that idea?"

"Don't try to pretend it isn't so! I—I have my sources of information. Peter, darling, why are you going?"

"I told you," he said, trying with only moderate success to put a flinty edge on his voice. "I'm an Earthman, not a colonist. I'm going home."

"Then I'll go with you! Darling, wait for me! Take me to Earth—I'll be your slave! I'm leaving now. I'll be at your villa in half an hour. Don't refuse me, Peter. I can't bear to lose you."

Martlett goggled and tried to reply, but before words would come out she had blanked the screen. He stared blearily at the sleek surface of the dead screen a moment, stunned. Coming here? In half an hour? But—

The phone chimed again.

With numbed fingers he activated it and watched the features of Sondra Bullard come swirling out of the electronic haze. She had heard he was leaving, she told him, and she implored him to change his mind. "Don't go," she begged him. "Stay right where you are. I'm on my way now. I have to see you again in person. I'll be there in half an hour. I love you, Peter."

"Half an hour? Aiee! Sondra—"

Too late. The screen was dead again.

Martlett remained quite still, sorting out the rush of thoughts that rippled through his chilled mind. They had both heard that he was leaving; that meant that most likely both, anticipating another runout à la Michael, had arranged with some underling of the secretary to be notified the moment he announced his intention to depart.

And they were on their way here to persuade him to change his mind. Joanne would be here in half an hour. Sondra would be here in half an hour. That meant—

He knew what that meant. They would *both* be here in half an hour. They were traveling on a collision orbit. And when they got together, critical mass would be reached rapidly.

Well, he thought in desperation, there was a clear path to safety still. All he had to do was report to the deserializing office *now*, and have them tuck him away in the Henderson Field until the midnight departure time. So far as it would matter to him, the elapsed time would be the same—hardly any at all—and he would be safely out of the reach of those grasping altar-eager females.

Martlett smiled. Yes, he thought. That's what I'll do!

He ordered the butler to get the jetcar ready for an immediate trip downtown. And in the meanwhile, he thought, there still is time for a drink. Something to calm my nerves. I paid two thousand units to settle Michael's liquor bills; I might as well enjoy some of it.

There was a liquor cabinet and dial bar at the opposite end of the living room. Martlett half skipped to it and quickly punched out an order for a double bourbon. Nothing happened; and then he recalled he had ordered the bar fixture disconnected that morning.

Shrugging, he tugged open the paneled door of the liquor cabinet and groped inside for one of the bottles. It was dim and dusty in there; he fumbled for a handhold, finally catching something—

He pulled.

What came out was not a bottle. He had been grasping a lever attached to a square black enamel box, and now box and lever both came out of the cabinet suddenly. He let go of the lever and jumped back. The box had popped open. "Damn," an oddly familiar voice said. "So soon?"

The box expanded abruptly. Martlett edged further back, and in the same moment a man stepped out of the box, stretching as if he had been crouching on his knees a long while and at last was standing up. He was tall—about Martlett's own height. He had unruly brown hair and a roguish smile, and a fine network of laugh wrinkles around his eyes.

He might almost have been Martlett's twin. He was, in point of fact, his younger brother.

He chuckled amiably and said, "Well, Peter—you're the last person I expected to see at this moment! "

Martlett backed up feebly. "Michael! You're—alive?"

"Extremely, dear brother. Would you mind telling me what year this is?"

Weakly, Martlett said, "2209. April 20th."

"Ha! The little vixens! Not even two months, and they've forgotten me already! Pfoo, it's dusty in here! What are *you* doing on Marathon, old man?"

In a chilly voice Martlett said, "After you were pronounced legally dead I was called here to serve as executor of your estate, Michael. I paid out some fourteen thousand units you owed. And now to find you're still alive! What—how—"

"I dare say you think it's ungrateful of me to come back to life, eh?" Michael smiled cozily. "Well, it was good of you to take care of the debts, Peter. This job did cost me a penny or two, and I'm afraid I rather neglected the tradesmen the while."

"What job? What are you talking about?"

"Why, the private Deserializer I had built, of course! "

Martlett put his hands to his head. He felt close to madness; the sudden arrival of his brother, the importuning of those girls, the fourteen thousand units, all seemed to swirl wildly around him. In a dark voice he said, "Will you explain yourself, Michael?"

"Certainly. There were these girls, you see—Joanne was the blonde, and Sondra the brunette."

"Yes, I know."

"Lovely, weren't they? Anyhow, with my usual carelessness I contrived to get myself engaged to both of them. It was an awkward situation; they both vowed to follow me to the ends of the universe, et cetera, the usual stuff. Damned tenacious lasses, both."

"I know that too," Martlett said.

"Do you, now? Well, to make the matter short," said Michael, "I found it expedient to disappear. I hired a person to arrange things for me, at a fee. He caused it to seem as if I had vanished in some awful way en route to Thermopylae or some such place in this system, when actually I hadn't even made the trip! I was deserialized and locked away in my own liquor closet, y'see, in cold storage, not conscious of the passage of time. There was a timer on the thing which would release me in five objective years—but you surely must know all about this?"

"On the contrary. It's quite new to me."

"But the arrangement was that my fellow would keep an eye on those two girls, and if they both got married before the five years were up he'd come around to let me out of the deserializer field right away. And since you've released me, then obviously—"

"No," Martlett said. "I pulled you out of the closet by accident. I thought you were dead."

"But I was only in there two months. And the girls—?"

"Still single. Both of them."

Michael's face turned paper white and he nibbled at his lips. "You mean they're both on the loose and you've released me? Oh, Peter, you incorrigible bungler! You—"

"Worse than that," Martlett interrupted. "They're both on their way here right now. They've decided to marry me, as long as you weren't available. They'll be here in—" he consulted his watch— "about four minutes, unless they happen to arrive early."

Michael was galvanized suddenly into frantic exertion. "Quick, then! I've got to leave here! If they ever find me alive they'll rip me to shreds! "

The butler suddenly rolled into the living room. It darted a confused glance from one Martlett brother to the other, and, its gears meshing and clanking in bewilderment, it announced, "Two ladies have just arrived to see Mr. Martlett."

"Tell them I'm not home! " Martlett and his brother shouted simultaneously.

"They insist on entering," the robot said.

Michael clutched at his brother's sleeve in panic. "What will we do?"

The outer doors were opening. The sound of agitated feminine conversation was audible outside. "Don't let them in," Michael ordered the butler. But the shock of seeing duplicate masters had put the robot out of commission; it drooled quietly to itself without obeying.

Martlett said in a voice heavy with defeat, "I guess we'll have to marry them, I suppose. Explain things first —we'll say you miraculously popped back into the continuum—and then marry them. We can't escape, Michael. And we *could* do worse for women, you know."

The voices were coming closer. "I guess you're right," Michael said. Lines of strain showed on his boyish face. "But—good grief, Peter! —*who marries which one?*"

Martlett shrugged. "Does it matter? I suppose we can toss for it."

Sounds reached them: *"Peter, darling, are you in there?"* And *"Who is this horrible woman, Peter?"*

Peter looked at his brother. It was the first time he had

131

ever seen Michael actually quaking with fear. "Stiff upper lip, boy," he muttered. "It shouldn't be so bad once you've explained."

"*You* explain," Michael said. "I don't dare."

"You'd better dare," Peter retorted. "You got us into this in the first place. You and your private Deserializer."

And there was no getting out, he thought, looking toward the door through which the girls were about to burst. They were trapped for fair. Might as well make the best of it.

Shoulder to shoulder, the Martlett brothers stood their ground and waited resignedly for the enemy to storm the battlements.

THE SIXTH PALACE

*Ben Azai was deemed worthy and stood at the gate of
the sixth palace and saw the ethereal splendor of the pure
marble plates. He opened his mouth and said twice,
"Water! Water!" In the twinkling of an eye they decapi-
tated him and threw eleven thousand iron bars at him.
This shall be a sign for all generations that no one should
err at the gate of the sixth palace.*

——Lesser Hekhaloth

There was the treasure, and there was the guardian of
the treasure. And there were the whitening bones of those
who had tried in vain to make the treasure their own.
Even the bones had taken on a kind of beauty, lying out
there by the gate of the treasure vault, under the blazing
arch of heavens. The treasure itself lent beauty to everything near it—even the scattered bones, even the grim
guardian.

The home of the treasure was a small world that belonged to red Valzar. Hardly more than moon-sized, really,
with no atmosphere to speak of, a silent, dead little world
that spun through darkness a billion miles from its cool-
ing primary. A wayfarer had stopped there once. Where
from, where bound? No one knew. He had established a
cache there, and there it still lay, changeless and eternal,
treasure beyond belief, presided over by the faceless metal

man who waited with metal patience for his master's return.

There were those who would have the treasure. They came, and were challenged by the guardian, and died.

On another world of the Valzar system, men undiscouraged by the fate of their predecessors dreamed of the hoard, and schemed to possess it. Lipescu was one: a tower of a man, golden beard, fists like hammers, gullet of brass, back as broad as a tree of a thousand years. Bolzano was another: awl-shaped, bright of eye, fast of finger, twig thick, razor sharp. They had no wish to die.

Lipescu's voice was like the rumble of island Galaxies in collision. He wrapped himself around a tankard of good black ale and said, "I go tomorrow, Bolzano."

"Is the computer ready?"

"Programed with everything the beast could ask me," the big man boomed. "There won't be a slip."

"And if there is?" Bolzano asked, peering idly into the blue, oddly pale, strangely meek eyes of the giant. "And if the robot kills you?"

"I've dealt with robots before."

Bolzano laughed. "That plain is littered with bones, friend. Yours will join the rest. Great bulky bones, Lipescu. I can see them now."

"You're a cheerful one, friend."

"I'm realistic."

Lipescu shook his head heavily. "If you were realistic, you wouldn't be in this with me," he said slowly. "Only a dreamer would do such a thing as this." One meaty paw hovered in the air, pounced, caught Bolzano's forearm. The little man winced as bones ground together. Lipescu said, "You won't back out? If I die, you'll make the attempt?"

"Of course I will, you idiot."

"Will you? You're a coward, like all little men. You'll watch me die, and then you'll turn tail and head for an-

134

other part of the universe as fast as you know how. Won't you?"

"I intend to profit by your mistakes," Bolzano said in a clear, testy voice. "Let go of my arm."

Lipescu released his grip. The little man sank back in his chair, rubbing his arm. He gulped ale. He grinned at his partner and raised his glass.

"To success," Bolzano said.

"Yes. To the treasure."

"And to long life afterward."

"For both of us," the big man boomed.

"Perhaps," said Bolzano. "Perhaps."

He had his doubts. The big man was sly, Ferd Bolzano knew, and that was a good combination, not often found: slyness and size. Yet the risks were great. Bolzano wondered which he preferred—that Lipescu should gain the treasure on his attempt, thus assuring Bolzano of a share without risk, or that Lipescu should die, forcing Bolzano to venture his own life. Which was better, a third of the treasure without hazard, or the whole thing for the highest stake?

Bolzano was good enough gambler to know the answer to that. Yet there was more than yellowness to the man; in his own way, he longed for the chance to risk his life on the airless treasure world.

Lipescu would go first. That was the agreement. Bolzano had stolen the computer, had turned it over to the big man, and Lipescu would make the initial attempt. If he gained the prize, his was the greater share. If he perished, it was Bolzano's moment next. An odd partnership, odd terms, but Lipescu would have it no other way, and Ferd Bolzano did not argue the point with his beefy compatriot. Lipescu would return with the treasure, or he would not return at all. There would be no middle way, they both were certain.

Bolzano spent an uneasy night. His apartment, in an airy shaft of a building overlooking glittering Lake Eris, was a comfortable place, and he had little longing to leave it. Lipescu, by preference, lived in the stinking slums beyond the southern shore of the lake, and when the two men parted for the night they went in opposite ways. Bolzano considered bringing a woman home for the night, but did not. Instead, he sat moody and wakeful before the televector screen, watching the procession of worlds, peering at the green and gold and ochre planets as they sailed through the emptiness.

Toward dawn, he ran the tape of the treasure. Octave Merlin had made that tape, a hundred years before, as he orbited sixty miles above the surface of the airless little world. Now Merlin's bones bleached on the plain, but the tape had come home, and bootlegged copies commanded a high price in hidden markets. His camera's sharp eye had seen much.

There was the gate; there was the guardian. Gleaming, ageless, splendid. The robot stood ten feet high, a square, blocky, black shape topped by the tiny anthroporphic head dome, featureless and sleek. Behind him the gate, wide open but impassable all the same. And behind him, the treasure, culled from the craftsmanship of a thousand worlds, left here who knew why, untold years ago.

No mere jewels. No dreary slabs of so-called precious metal. The wealth here was not intrinsic; no vandal would think of melting the treasure into dead ingots. Here were statuettes of spun iron, that seemed to move and breathe. Plaques of purest lead, engraved with lathework that dazzled the mind and made the heart hesitate. Cunning intaglios in granite, from the workshops of a frosty world half a parsec from nowhere. A scatter of opals, burning with an inner light, fashioned into artful loops of brightness.

A helix of rainbow-colored wood. A series of interlock-

136

ing strips of some beast's bone, bent and splayed so that the pattern blurred and perhaps abutted some other-dimensional continuum. Cleverly carved shells, one within the other, descending to infinity. Burnished leaves of nameless trees. Polished pebbles from unknown beaches. A dizzying spew of wonders, covering some fifty square yards, sprawled out behind the gate in stunning profusion.

Rough men unschooled in the tenets of esthetics had given their lives to possess the treasure. It took no fancy knowledge to realize the wealth of it, to know that collectors strung from Galaxy to Galaxy would fight with bared fangs to claim their share. Gold bars did not a treasure make. But these things? Beyond duplication, almost beyond price?

Bolzano was wet with a fever of yearning before the tape had run its course. When it was over, he slumped in his chair, drained, depleted.

Dawn came, The silvery moons fell from the sky. The red sun splashed across the heavens. Bolzano allowed himself the luxury of an hour's sleep.

And then it was time to begin. . . .

As a precautionary measure, they left the ship in a parking orbit three miles above the airless world. Past reports were unreliable, and there was no telling how far the robot guardian's power extended. If Lipescu were successful, Bolzano could descend and get him—and the treasure. If Lipescu failed, Bolzano would land and make his own attempt.

The big man looked even bigger, encased in his suit and in the outer casement of a dropshaft. Against his massive chest he wore the computer, an extra brain as lovingly crafted as any object in the treasure hoard. The guardian would ask him questions; the computer would help him answer. And Bolzano would listen. If Lipescu erred, possibly his partner could benefit by knowledge of the error and succeed.

"Can you hear me?" Lipescu asked.

"Perfectly. Go on, get going! "

"What's the hurry? Eager to see me die?"

"Are you that lacking in confidence?" Bolzano asked. "Do you want me to go first?"

"Fool," Lipescu muttered. "Listen carefully. If I die, I don't want it to be in vain."

"What would it matter to you?"

The bulky figure wheeled around. Bolzano could not see his partner's face, but he knew Lipescu must be scowling. The giant rumbled, "Is life that valuable? Can't I take a risk?"

"For *my* benefit?"

"For mine," Lipescu said. "I'll be coming back."

"Go, then. The robot is waiting."

Lipescu walked to the lock. A moment later he was through and gliding downward, a one-man spaceship, jets flaring beneath his feet. Bolzano settled by the scanner to watch. A televector pickup homed in on Lipescu just as he made his landing, coming down in a blaze of fire. The treasure and its guardian lay about a mile away. Lipescu rid himself of the dropshaft, stepping with giant bounds toward the waiting guardian.

Bolzano watched.

Bolzano listened.

The televector pickup provided full fidelity. It was useful for Bolzano's purposes, and useful, too, for Lipescu's vanity, for the big man wanted his every moment taped for posterity. It was interesting to see Lipescu dwarfed by the guardian. The black faceless robot, squat and motionless, topped the big man by better than three feet.

Lipescu said, "Step aside."

The robot's reply came in surprisingly human tones,

though void of any distinguishing accent. "What I guard is not to be plundered."

"I claim them by right," Lipescu said.

"So have many others. But their right did not exist. Nor does yours. I cannot step aside for you."

"Test me," Lipescu said. "See if I have the right or not! "

"Only my master may pass."

"Who is your master? *I* am your master! "

"My master is he who can command me. And no one can command me who shows ignorance before me."

"Test me, then," Lipescu demanded.

"Death is the penalty for failure."

"Test me."

"The treasure does not belong to you."

"Test me and step aside."

"Your bones will join the rest here."

"Test me," Lipescu said.

Watching from aloft, Bolzano went tense. His thin body drew together like that of a chilled spider. Anything might happen now. The robot might propound riddles, like the Sphinx confronting Oedipus.

It might demand the proofs of mathematical theorems. It might ask the translation of strange words. So they gathered, from their knowledge of what had befallen other men here. And, so it seemed, to give a wrong answer was to earn instant death.

He and Lipescu had ransacked the libraries of the world. They had packed all knowledge, so they hoped, into their computer. It had taken months, even with multi-stage programing. The tiny shining globe of metal on Lipescu's chest contained an infinity of answers to an infinity of questions.

Below, there was long silence as man and robot studied one another. Then the guardian said, "Define latitude."

"Do you mean geographical latitude?" Lipescu asked.

139

Bolzano congealed with fear. The idiot, asking for a clarification! He would die before he began!

The robot said, "Define latitude."

Lipescu's voice was calm. "The angular distance of a point on a planet's surface north or south of the equator, as measured from the center of the planet."

"Which is more consonant," the robot asked, "the minor third or the major sixth?"

There was a pause. Lipescu was no musician. But the computer would feed him the answer.

"The minor third," Lipescu said.

Without a pause, the robot fired another question. "Name the prime numbers between 5,237 and 7, 641."

Bolzano smiled as Lipescu handled the question with ease. So far, so good. The robot had stuck to strictly factual questions, schoolbook stuff, posing no real problems to Lipescu. And after the initial hesitation and quibble over latitude, Lipescu had seemed to grow in confidence from moment to moment. Bolzano squinted at the scanner, looking beyond the robot, through the open gate, to the helter-skelter pile of treasures. He wondered which would fall to his lot when he and Lipescu divided them, two-thirds for Lipescu, the rest for him.

"Name the seven tragic poets of Elifora," the robot said.

"Domiphar, Halionis, Slegg, Hork-Sekan—"

"The fourteen signs of the zodiac as seen from Morneez," the robot demanded.

"The Teeth, the Serpents, the Leaves, the Waterfall, the Blot—"

"What is a pedicel?"

"The stalk of an individual flower of an inflorescence."

"How many years did the Siege of Larrina last?"

"Eight."

"What did the flower cry in the third canto of Somner's *Vehicles*?"

"I ache, I sob, I whimper, I die," Lipescu boomed.

"Distinguish between the stamen and the pistil."

"The stamen is the pollen-producing organ of the flower; the pistil—"

And so it went. Question after question. The robot was not content with the legendary three questions of mythology; it asked a dozen, and then asked more. Lipsecu answered perfectly, prompted by the murmuring of the peerless compendium of knowledge strapped to his chest. Bolzano kept careful count: The big man had dealt magnificently with seventeen questions. When would the robot concede defeat? When would it end its grim quiz and step aside?

It asked an eighteenth question, pathetically easy. All it wanted was an exposition of the Pythagorean Theorem. Lipsecu did not even need the computer for that. He answered, briefly, concisely, correctly. Bolzano was proud of his burly partner.

Then the robot struck Lipescu dead.

It happened in the flickering of an eyelid. Lipescu's voice had ceased, and he stood there, ready for the next question, but the next question did not come. Rather, a panel in the robot's vaulted bellys slid open, and something bright and sinuous lashed out, uncoiling over the ten feet or so that separated guardian from challenger, and sliced Lipescu in half. The bright something slid back out of sight. Lipescu's trunk toppled to one side. His massive legs remained absurdly planted for a moment; then they crumpled, and a spacesuited leg kicked once, and all was still.

Stunned, Bolzano trembled in the loneliness of the cabin, and his lymph turned to water. What had gone wrong? Lipescu had given the proper answer to every question, and yet the robot had slain him. Why? Could the big man possibly have misphrased Pythagoras? No: Bolzano, had listened. The answer had been flawless, as had the seventeen that preceded it. Seemingly the robot had lost patience with the game, then. The robot had cheated. Arbitrarily, maliciously, it had lashed out at Lipescu, punishing him for the correct answer.

Did robots cheat, Bolzano wondered? Could they act in malicious spite? No robot he knew was capable of such actions; but this robot was unlike all others.

For a long while, Bolzano remained huddled in the cabin. The temptation was strong to blast free of orbit and head home, treasureless but alive. Yet the treasure called to him. Some suicidal impulse drove him on. Sirenlike, the robot drew him downward.

There had to be a way to make the robot yield, Bolzano thought, as he guided his small ship down to the broad barren plain. Using the computer had been a good idea, whose only defect was that it hadn't worked. The records were uncertain, but it appeared that in the past men had died when they finally gave a wrong answer after a series of right ones. Lipescu had given no wrong answers. Yet he too had died. It was inconceivable that the robot understood some relationship of the squares on the hypotenuse and on the other two sides that was different from the relationship Lipescu had expressed.

Bolzano wondered what method would work.

He plodded leadenly across the plain toward the gate and its guardian. The germ of an idea formed in him, as he walked doggedly on.

He was, he knew, condemned to death by his own greed. Only extreme agility of mind would save him from sharing Lipescu's fate. Ordinary intelligence would not work. Odyssean cleverness was the only salvation.

Bolzano approached the robot. Bones lay everywhere. Lipescu weltered in his own blood. Against that vast dead chest lay the computer, Bolzano knew. But he shrank from

142

reaching for it. He would do without it. He looked away, unwilling to let the sight of Lipescu's severed body interfere with the coolness of his thoughts.

He collected his courage. The robot showed no interest in him.

"Give ground," Bolzano said. "I am here. I come for the treasure."

"Win your right to it."

"What must I do?"

"Demonstrate truth," the robot said. "Reveal inwardness. Display understanding."

"I am ready," said Bolzano.

The robot offered a question. "What is the excretory unit of the vertebrate kidney called?"

Bolzano contemplated. He had no idea. The computer could tell him, but the computer lay strapped to fallen Lipescu. No matter. The robot wanted truth, inwardness, understanding. Those things were not necessarily the same as information. Lipescu had offered information. Lipescu had perished.

"The frog in the pond," Bolzano said, "utters an azure cry."

There was silence. Bolzano watched the robot's front, waiting for the panel to slide open, the sinuous something to chop him in half.

The robot said, "During the War of Dogs on Vanderveer IX, the embattled colonists drew up thirty-eight dogmas of defiance. Quote the third, the ninth, the twenty-second, and the thirty-fifth."

Bolzano pondered. This was an alien robot, product of an unknown hand. How did its maker's mind work? Did it respect knowledge? Did it treasure facts for their own sake? Or did it recognize that information is meaningless, insight a nonlogical process?

Lipescu had been logical. He lay in pieces.

143

"The mereness of pain," Bolzano responded, "is ineffable and refreshing."

The robot said, "The monastery of Kwaisen was besieged by the soldiers of Oda Nobunaga on the third of April, 1582. What words of wisdom did the abbot utter?"

Bolzano spoke quickly and buoyantly. "Eleven, forty-one, elephant, voluminous."

The last word slipped from his lips despite an effort to retrieve it. Elephants *were* voluminous, he thought. A fatal slip? The robot did not appear to notice.

Sonorously ponderously, the great machine delivered the next question.

"What is the percentage of oxygen in the atmosphere of Muldonar VII?"

"False witness bears a swift sword," Bolzano replied.

The robot made an odd humming sound. Abruptly it rolled on massive treads, moving some six feet to its left. The gate of the treasure trove stood wide, beckoning.

"You may enter," the robot said.

Bolzano's heart leaped. He had won! He had gained the high prize!

Others had failed, most recently less than an hour before, and their bones glistened on the plain. They had tried to answer the robot, sometimes giving right answers, sometimes giving wrong ones, and they had died. Bolzano lived.

It was a miracle, he thought. Luck? Shrewdness? Some of each, he told himself. He had watched a man give eighteen right answers and die. So the accuracy of the responses did not matter to the robot. What did? Inwardness. Understanding. Truth.

There could be inwardness and understanding and truth in random answers, Bolzano realized. Where earnest striving had failed, mockery had succeeded. He had staked his life on nonsense, and the prize was his.

He staggered forward, into the treasure trove. Even in the light gravity, his feet were like leaden weights. Tension ebbed in him. He knelt among the treasures.

The tapes, the sharp-eyed televector scanners, had not begun to indicate the splendor of what lay here. Bolzano stared in awe and rapture at a tiny disk, no greater in diameter than a man's eye, on which myriad coiling lines writhed and twisted in patterns of rare beauty. He caught his breath, sobbing with the pain of perception as a gleaming marble spire, angled in mysterious swerves, came into view. Here, a bright beetle of some fragile waxy substance rested on a pedestal of yellow jade. There, a tangle of metallic cloth spurted dizzying patterns of luminescence. And over there—and beyond—and there—

The ransom of a universe, Bolzano thought.

It would take many trips to carry all this to his ship. Perhaps it would be better to bring the ship to the hoard, eh? He wondered, though, if he would lose his advantage if he stepped back through the gate. Was it possible that he would have to win entrance all over again? And would the robot accept his answers as willingly the second time?

It was something he would have to chance, Bolzano decided. His nimble mind worked out a plan. He would select a dozen, two dozen of the finest treasures, as much as he could comfortably carry, and take them back to the ship. Then he would lift the ship and set it down next to the gate. If the robot raised objections about his entering, Bolzano would simply depart, taking what he had already secured. There was no point in running undue risks. When he had sold this cargo, and felt pinched for money, he could always return and try to win admission once again. Certainly, no one else would steal the horde if he abandoned it.

Selection, that was the key now.

Crouching, Bolzano picked through the treasure, choosing for portability and easy marketability. The marble spire? Too big. But the coiling disk, yes, certainly, and the beetle, of course, and this small statuette of dull hue, and the cameos showing scenes no human eye had ever beheld, and this, and this, and this—

His pulse raced. His heart thundered. He saw himself traveling from world to world, vending his wares. Collectors, museums, governments would vie with one another to have these prizes. He would let them bid each object up into the millions before he sold. And, of course, he would keep one or two for himself—or perhaps three or four—souvenirs of this great adventure.

And someday when wealth bored him he would return and face the challenge again. And he would dare the robot to question him, and he would reply with random absurdities, demonstrating his grasp on the fundamental insight that in knowledge there is only hollow merit, and the robot would admit him once more to the treasure trove.

Bolzano rose. He cradled his lovelies in his arms. Carefully, carefully, he thought. Turning, he made his way through the gate.

The robot had not moved. It had shown no interest as Bolzano plundered the hoard. The small man walked calmly past it.

The robot said, "Why have you taken those? What do you want with them?"

Bolzano smiled. Nonchalantly he replied, "I've taken them because they're beautiful. Because I want them. Is there a better reason?"

"No," the robot said, and the panel slid open in its ponderous black chest.

Too late, Bolzano realized that the test had not yet ended, that the robot's question had arisen out of no idle

146

curiosity. And this time he had replied in earnest, speaking in rational terms.

Bolzano shrieked. He saw the brightness coming toward him.

Death followed instantly.

TO SEE THE INVISIBLE MAN

And then they found me guilty, and then they pronounced me invisible, for a span of one year beginning on the eleventh of May in the year of Grace 2104, and they took me to a dark room beneath the courthouse to affix the mark to my forehead before turning me loose.

Two municipally paid ruffians did the job. One flung me into a chair and the other lifted the brand.

"This won't hurt a bit," the slab-jawed ape said, and thrust the brand against my forehead, and there was a moment of coolness, and that was all.

"What happens now?" I asked.

But there was no answer, and they turned away from me and left the room without a word. The door remained open. I was free to leave, or to stay and rot, as I chose. No one would speak to me, or look at me more than once, long enough to see the sign on my forehead. I was invisible.

You must understand that my invisibility was strictly metaphorical. I still had corporeal solidity. People *could* see me—but they *would not* see me.

An absurd punishment? Perhaps. But then, the crime was absurd too. The crime of coldness. Refusal to un-burden myself for my fellow man. I was a four-time offender. The penalty for that was a year's invisibility.

The complaint had been duly sworn, the trial held, the brand duly affixed.

I was invisible.

I went out, out into the world of warmth.

They had already had the afternoon rain. The streets of the city were drying, and there was the smell of growth in the Hanging Gardens. Men and women went about their business. I walked among them, but they took no notice of me.

The penalty for speaking to an invisible man is invisibility, a month to a year or more, depending on the seriousness of the offense. On this the whole concept depends. I wondered how rigidly the rule was observed.

I soon found out.

I stepped into a liftshaft and let myself be spiraled up toward the nearest of the Hanging Gardens. It was Eleven, the cactus garden, and those gnarled, bizarre shapes suited my mood. I emerged on the landing stage and advanced toward the admission counter to buy my token. A pasty-faced, empty-eyed woman sat back of the counter.

I laid down my coin. Something like fright entered her eyes, quickly faded.

"One admission," I said.

No answer. People were queueing up behind me. I repeated my demand. The woman looked up helplessly, then stared over my left shoulder. A hand extended itself, another coin was placed down. She took it, and handed the man his token. He dropped it in the slot and went in.

"Let me have a token," I said crisply.

Others were jostling me out of the way. Not a word of apology. I began to sense some of the meaning of my invisibility. They were literally treating me as though they could not see me.

There are countervailing advantages. I walked around behind the counter and helped myself to a token without paying for it. Since I was invisible, I could not be stopped. I thrust the token in the slot and entered the garden.

But the cacti bored me. An inexpressible malaise slipped over me, and I felt no desire to stay. On my way out I pressed my finger against a jutting thorn and drew blood. The cactus, at least, still recognized my existence. But only to draw blood.

I returned to my apartment. My books awaited me, but I felt no interest in them. I sprawled out on my narrow bed and activated the energizer to combat the strange lassitude that was afflicting me. I thought about my invisibility.

It would not be such a hardship, I told myself. I had never depended overly on other human beings. Indeed, had I not been sentenced in the first place for my coldness toward my fellow creatures? So what need did I have of them now? *Let* them ignore me!

It would be restful. I had a year's respite from work, after all. Invisible men did not work. How could they? Who would go to an invisible doctor for a consultation, or hire an invisible lawyer to represent him, or give a document to an invisible clerk to file? No work, then. No income, of course, either. But landlords did not take rent from invisible men. Invisible men went where they pleased, at no cost. I had just demonstrated that at the Hanging Gardens.

Invisibility would be a great joke on society, I felt. They had sentenced me to nothing more dreadful than a year's rest cure. I was certain I would enjoy it.

But there were certain practical disadvantages. On the first night of my invisibility I went to the city's finest restaurant. I would order their most lavish dishes, a hundred-unit meal, and then conveniently vanish at the presentation of the bill.

My thinking was muddy. I never got seated. I stood in

150

the entrance half an hour, bypassed again and again by a maitre d'hotel who had clearly been through all this many times before. Walking to a seat, I realized, would gain me nothing. No waiter would take my order.

I could go into the kitchen. I could help myself to anything I pleased. I could disrupt the workings of the restaurant. But I decided against it. Society had its ways of protecting itself against invisible ones. There could be no direct retaliation, of course, no intentional defense. But who could say no to a chef's claim that he had seen no one in the way when he hurled a pot of scalding water toward the wall? Invisibility was invisibility, a two-edged sword.

I left the restaurant.

I ate at an automated restaurant nearby. Then I took an autocab home. Machines, like cacti, did not discriminate against my sort. I sensed that they would make poor companions for a year, though.

I slept poorly.

The second day of my invisibility was a day of further testing and discovery.

I went for a long walk, careful to stay on the pedestrian paths. I had heard all about the boys who enjoy running down those who carry the mark of invisibility on their foreheads. Again, there is no recourse, no punishment for them. My condition has its little hazards by intention.

I walked the streets, seeing how the throngs parted for me. I cut through them like a microtome passing between cells. They were well trained. At midday I saw my first fellow Invisible. He was a tall man of middle years, stocky and dignified, bearing the mark of shame on a domelike forehead. His eyes met mine only for a moment. Then he passed on. An invisible man, naturally, cannot see another of his kind.

I was amused, nothing more. I was still savoring the

151

novelty of this way of life. No slight could hurt me. Not yet.

Late in the day I came to one of those bathhouses where working girls can cleanse themselves for a couple of small coins. I smiled wickedly and went up the steps. The attendant at the door gave me the flicker of a startled look—it was a small triumph for me—but did not dare to stop me.

I went in.

An overpowering smell of soap and sweat struck me. I persevered inward. I passed cloakrooms where long rows of gray smocks were hanging, and it occurred to me that I could rifle those smocks of every unit they contained, but I did not. Theft loses meaning when it becomes too easy, as the clever ones who devised invisibility were aware.

I passed on, into the bath chambers themselves.

Hundreds of women were there. Nubile girls, weary wenches, old crones. Some blushed. A few smiled. Many turned their backs on me. But they were careful not to show any real reaction to my presence. Supervisory matrons stood guard, and who knew but that she might be reported for taking undue cognizance of the existence of an Invisible?

So I watched them bathe, watched five hundred pairs of bobbing breasts, watched naked bodies glistening under the spray, watched this vast mass of bare feminine flesh. My reaction was a mixed one, a sense of wicked achievement at having penetrated this sanctum sanctorum unhalted, and then, welling up slowly within me, a sensation of—was it sorrow? Boredom? Revulsion?

I was unable to analyze it. But it felt as though a clammy hand had seized my throat. I left quickly. The smell of soapy water stung my nostrils for hours afterward, and the sight of pink flesh haunted my dreams that night. I ate alone, in one of the automatics. I began to see that the novelty of this punishment was soon lost.

In the third week I fell ill. It began with a high fever, then pains of the stomach, vomiting, the rest of the ugly symptomatology. By midnight I was certain I was dying. The cramps were intolerable, and when I dragged myself to the toilet cubicle I caught sight of my face in the mirror, distorted, greenish, beaded with sweat. The mark of invisibility stood out like a beacon in my pale forehead.

For a long time I lay on the tiled floor, limply absorbing the coolness of it. Then I thought: What if it's my appendix? That ridiculous, obsolete, obscure prehistoric survival? Inflamed, ready to burst?

I needed a doctor.

The phone was covered with dust. They had not bothered to disconnect it, but I had not called anyone since my arrest, and no one had dared call me. The penalty for knowingly telephoning an invisible man is invisibility. My friends, such as they were, had stayed far away.

I grasped the phone, thumbed the panel. It lit up and the directory robot said, "With whom do you wish to speak, sir?"

"Doctor," I gasped.

"Certainly, sir." Bland, smug mechanical words! No way to pronounce a robot invisible, so it was free to talk to me!

The screen glowed. A doctorly voice said, "What seems to be the trouble?"

"Stomach pains. Maybe appendicitis."

"We'll have a man over in—" He stopped. I had made the mistake of upturning my agonized face. His eyes lit on my forehead mark. The screen winked into blackness as rapidly as though I had extended a leprous hand for him to kiss.

"Doctor," I groaned.

He was gone. I buried my face in my hands. This was

153

carrying things too far, I thought. Did the Hippocratic Oath allow things like this? Could a doctor ignore a sick man's plea for help?

Hippocrates had not known anything about invisible men. A doctor was not required to minister to an invisible man. To society at large I simply was not there. Doctors could not diagnose diseases in nonexistent individuals.

I was left to suffer.

It was one of invisibility's less attractive features. You enter a bathhouse unhindered, if that pleases you—but you writhe on a bed of pain equally unhindered. The one with the other, and if your appendix happens to rupture, why, it is all the greater deterrent to others who might perhaps have gone your lawless way!

My appendix did not rupture. I survived, though badly shaken. A man can survive without human conversation for a year. He can travel on automated cars and eat at automated restaurants. But there are no automated doctors. For the first time, I felt truly beyond the pale. A convict in a prison is given a doctor when he falls ill. My crime had not been serious enough to merit prison, and so no doctor would treat me if I suffered. It was unfair. I cursed the devils who had invented my punishment. I faced each bleak dawn alone, as alone as Crusoe on his island, here in the midst of a city of twelve million souls.

How can I describe my shifts of mood, my many tacks before the changing winds of the passing months?

There were times when invisibility was a joy, a delight, a treasure. In those paranoid moments I gloried in my exemption from the rules that bound ordinary men.

I stole. I entered small stores and seized the receipts while the cowering merchant feared to stop me, lest in crying out he make himself liable to my invisibility. If I had known that the State reimbursed all such losses, I might have taken less pleasure in it. But I stole.

154

I invaded. The bathhouses never tempted me again, but I breached other sanctuaries. I entered hotels and walked down the corridors, opening doors at random. Most rooms were empty. Some were not.

Godlike, I observed all. I toughened. My disdain for society—the crime that had earned me invisibility in the first place—heightened.

I stood in the empty streets during the periods of rain, and railed at the gleaming faces of the towering buildings on every side. "Who needs you?" I roared. "Not I! Who needs you in the slightest?"

I jeered and mocked and railed. It was a kind of insanity, brought on, I suppose, by the loneliness. I entered theaters —where the happy lotus eaters sat slumped in their massage chairs, transfixed by the glowing tridim images—and capered down the aisles. No one grumbled at me. The luminescence of my forehead told them to keep their complaints to themselves, and they did.

Those were the mad moments, the good moments, the moments when I towered twenty feet high and strode among the visible clods with contempt oozing from every pore. Those were insane moments—I admit that freely. A man who has been in a condition of involuntary invisibility for several months is not likely to be well balanced.

Did I call them paranoid moments? Manic depressive might be more to the point. The pendulum swung dizzily. The days when I felt only contempt for the visible fools all around me were balanced by days when the isolation pressed in tangibly on me. I would walk the endless streets, pass through the gleaming arcades, stare down at the highways with their streaking bullets of gay colors. Not even a beggar would come up to me. Did you know we had beggars, in our shining century? Not till I was pronounced invisible did I know it, for then my long walks took me to the slums, where the shine has worn thin,

155

and where shuffling stubble-faced old men beg for small coins.

No one begged for coins from me. Once a blind man came up to me.

"For the love of God," he wheezed, "help me to buy new eyes from the eye bank."

They were the first direct words any human being had spoken to me in months. I started to reach into my tunic for money, planning to give him every unit on me in gratitude. Why not? I could get more simply by taking it. But before I could draw the money out, a nightmare figure hobbled on crutches between us. I caught the whispered word, "Invisible," and then the two of them scuttled away like frightened crabs. I stood there stupidly holding my money.

Not even the beggars. Devils, to have invented this torment!

So I softened again. My arrogance ebbed away. I was lonely, now. Who could accuse me of coldness? I was spongy soft, pathetically eager for a word, a smile, a clasping hand. It was the sixth month of my invisibility.

I loathed it entirely, now. Its pleasures were hollow ones and its torment was unbearable. I wondered how I would survive the remaining six months. Believe me, suicide was not far from my mind in those dark hours.

And finally I committed an act of foolishness. On one of my endless walks I encountered another Invisible, no more than the third or the fourth such creature I had seen in my six months. As in the previous encounters, our eyes met, warily, only for a moment. Then he dropped his to the pavement, and he sidestepped me and walked on. He was a slim young man, no more than forty, with touseled brown hair, and a narrow, pinched face. He had a look of scholarship about him, and I wondered what he might have done to merit his punishment, and I was seized with the desire to run after him and ask him, and to learn his name, and talk to him, and embrace him.

All these things are forbidden to mankind. No one shall have any contact whatsoever with an Invisible—not even a fellow Invisible. Especially not a fellow Invisible. There is no wish on society's part to foster a secret bond of fellowship among its pariahs.

I knew all this.

I turned and followed him, all the same.

For three blocks I moved along behind him, remaining twenty to fifty paces to the rear. Security robots seemed to be everywhere, their scanners quick to detect an infraction, and I did not dare make my move. Then he turned down a side street, a gray, dusty street five centuries old, and began to stroll, with the ambling, going-nowhere gait of the Invisible. I came up behind him.

"Please," I said softly. "No one will see us here. We can talk. My name is—"

He whirled on me, horror in his eyes. His face was pale. He looked at me in amazement for a moment, then darted forward as though to go around me.

I blocked him.

"Wait," I said. "Don't be afraid. Please—"

He burst past me. I put my hand on his shoulder, and he wriggled free.

"Just a word," I begged.

Not even a word. Not even a hoarsely uttered, "Leave me alone!" He sidestepped me and ran down the empty street, his steps diminishing from a clatter to a murmur as he reached the corner and rounded it. I looked after him, feeling a great loneliness well up in me.

And then a fear. *He* hadn't breached the rules of invisibility, but I had. I had seen him. That left me subject to punishment, an extension of my term of invisibility, perhaps. I looked around anxiously, but there were no security robots in sight, no one at all.

I was alone.

Turning, calming myself, I continued down the street. Gradually I regained control over myself. I saw that I had done something unpardonably foolish. The stupidity of my action troubled me, but even more the sentimentality of it. To reach out in that panicky way to another Invisible—to admit openly my loneliness, my need—no. It meant that society was winning. I couldn't have that.

I found that I was near the cactus garden once again. I rode the liftshaft, grabbed a token from the attendant, and bought my way in. I searched for a moment, then found a twisted, elaborately ornate cactus eight feet high, a spiny monster. I wrenched it from its pot and broke the angular limbs to fragments, filling my hands with a thousand needles. People pretended not to watch. I plucked the spines from my hands and, palms bleeding, rode the liftshaft down, once again sublimely aloof in my invisibility.

The eighth month passed, the ninth, the tenth. The seasonal round had made nearly a complete turn. Spring had given way to a mild summer, summer to a crisp autumn, autumn to winter with its fortnightly snowfalls, still permitted for esthetic reasons. Winter had ended, now. In the parks, the trees sprouted green buds. The weather control people stepped up the rainfall to thrice daily.

My term was drawing to its end.

In the final months of my invisibility I had slipped into a kind of torpor. My mind, forced back on its own resources, no longer cared to consider the implications of my condition, and I slid in a blurred haze from day to day. I read compulsively but unselectively. Aristotle one day, the Bible the next, a handbook of mechanics the next. I retained nothing; as I turned a fresh page, its predecessor slipped from my memory.

158

I no longer bothered to enjoy the few advantages of invisibility, the voyeuristic thrills, the minute throb of power that comes from being able to commit any act with only limited fear of retaliation. I say *limited* because the passage of the Invisibility Act had not been accompanied by an act repealing human nature; few men would not risk invisibility to protect their wives or children from an invisible one's molestations; no one would coolly allow an Invisible to jab out his eyes; no one would tolerate an Invisible's invasion of his home. There were ways of coping with such infringements without appearing to recognize the existence of the Invisible, as I have mentioned.

Still, it was possible to get away with a great deal. I declined to try. Somewhere Dostoeivski has written, "Without God, all things are possible." I can amend that. "To the invisible man, all things are possible—and uninteresting." So it was.

The weary months passed.

I did not count the minutes till my release. To be precise, I wholly forgot that my term was due to end. On the day itself, I was reading in my room, morosely turning page after page, when the annunciator chimed.

It had not chimed for a full year. I had almost forgotten the meaning of the sound.

But I opened the door. There they stood, the men of the law. Wordlessly, they broke the seal that held the mark to my forehead. The emblem dropped away and shattered.

"Hello, citizen," they said to me.

I nodded gravely. "Yes. Hello."

"May 11, 2105. Your term is up. You are restored to society. You have paid your debt."

"Thank you. Yes."

"Come for a drink with us."

"I'd sooner not."

"It's the tradition. Come along."

I went with them. My forehead felt strangely naked now, and I glanced in a mirror to see that there was a pale spot where the emblem had been. They took me to a bar nearby, and treated me to synthetic whiskey, raw, powerful. The bartender grinned at me. Someone on the next stool clapped me on the shoulder and asked me who I liked in tomorrow's jet races. I had no idea, and I said so.

"You mean it? I'm backing Kelso. Four to one, but he's got terrific spurt power."

"I'm sorry," I said.

"He's been away for a while," one of the government men said softly.

The euphemism was unmistakable. My neighbor glanced at my forehead and nodded at the pale spot. He offered to buy me a drink too. I accepted, though I was already feeling the effects of the first one. I was a human being again. I was visible.

I did not dare snub him, anyway. It might have been construed as the crime of coldness once again. My fifth offense would have meant five years of Invisibility. I had learned humility.

Returning to visibility involved an awkward transition, of course. Old friends to meet, lame conversations to hold, shattered relationships to renew. I had been an exile in my own city for a year, and coming back was not easy.

No one referred to my time of invisibility, naturally. It was treated as an affliction best left unmentioned. Hypocrisy, I thought, but I accepted it. Doubtless they were all trying to spare my feelings. Does one tell a man whose cancerous stomach has been replaced, "I hear you had a narrow escape just now?" Does one say to a man whose aged father has tottered off toward a euthanasia house,

160

"Well, he was getting pretty feeble anyway, wasn't he?"

No. Of course not.

So there was this hole in our shared experience, this void, this blankness. Which left me little to talk about with my friends, in particular since I had lost the knack of conversation entirely. The period of readjustment was a trying one.

But I persevered, for I was no longer the same haughty, aloof person I had been before my conviction. I had learned humility in the hardest of schools.

Now and then I noticed an Invisible on the streets, of course. It was impossible to avoid them. But, trained as I had been trained, I quickly glanced away, as though my eyes had come momentarily to rest on some shambling, festering horror from another world.

It was in the fourth month of my return to visibility that the ultimate lesson of my sentence struck home, though. I was in the vicinity of the City Tower, having returned to my old job in the documents division of the municipal government. I had left work for the day and was walking toward the tubes when a hand emerged from the crowd, caught my arm.

"Please," the soft voice said. "Wait a minute. Don't be afraid."

I looked up, startled. In our city strangers do not accost strangers.

I saw the gleaming emblem of invisibility on the man's forehead. Then I recognized him—the slim boy I had accosted more than half a year before on that deserted street. He had grown haggard; his eyes were wild, his brown hair flecked with gray. He must have been at the beginning of his term, then. Now he must have been near its end.

He held my arm. I trembled. This was no deserted street. This was the most crowded square of the city. I pulled my arm away from his grasp and started to turn away.

161

"No—don't go," he cried. "Can't you pity me? You've been there yourself."

I took a faltering step. Then I remembered how I had cried out to him, how I had begged him not to spurn me. I remembered my own miserable loneliness.

I took another step away from him.

"Coward! " he shrieked after me. "Talk to me! I dare you! Talk to me, coward! "

It was too much. I was touched. Sudden tears stung my eyes, and I turned to him, stretched out a hand to his. I caught his thin wrist. The contact seemed to electrify him. A moment later, I held him in my arms, trying to draw some of the misery from his frame to mine.

The security robots closed in, surrounding us. He was hurled to one side, I was taken into custody. They will try me again—not for the crime of coldness, this time, but for a crime of warmth. Perhaps they will find extenuating circumstances and release me; perhaps not.

I do not care. If they condemn me, this time I will wear my invisibility like a shield of glory.

THE IRON CHANCELLOR

The Carmichaels were a pretty plump family, to begin with. Not one of the four of them couldn't stand to shed quite a few pounds. And there happened to be a superspecial on roboservitors at one of the Miracle Mile roboshops— 40% off on the 2061 model, with adjustable caloric-intake monitors.

Sam Carmichael liked the idea of having his food prepared and served by a robot who would keep one beady solenoid eye on the collective family waistline. He squinted speculatively at the glossy display model, absentmindedly slipped his thumbs beneath his elastobelt to knead his paunch, and said, "How much?"

The salesman flashed a brilliant and probably synthetic grin. "Only 2995, sir. That includes free service contract for the first five years. Only two hundred credits down and up to forty months to pay."

Carmichael frowned, thinking of his bank balance. Then he thought of his wife's figure, and of his daughter's endless yammering about her need to diet. Besides, Jemima, their old robocook, was shabby and gear-stripped, and made a miserable showing when other company executives visited them for dinner.

"I'll take it," he said.

"Care to trade in your old robocook, sir? Liberal trade-in allowances—"

"I have a '43 Madison." Carmichael wondered if he

should mention its bad arm libration and serious fuel-feed overflow, but decided that would be carrying candidness too far.

"Well—ah—I guess we could allow you fifty credits on a '43, sir. Seventy-five, maybe, if the recipe bank is still in good condition."

"Excellent condition." That part was honest—the family had never let even one recipe wear out. "You could send a man down to look her over."

"Oh, no need to do that, sir. We'll take your word. Seventy-five, then? And delivery of the new model by this evening?"

"Done," Carmichael said. He was glad to get the pathetic old '43 out of the house at any cost.

He signed the purchase order cheerfully, pocketed the facsim and handed over ten crisp twenty-credit vouchers. He could almost feel the roll of fat melting from him now, as he eyed the magnificent '61 roboservitor that would shortly be his.

The time was only 1810 hours when he left the shop, got into his car and punched out the coordinates for home. The whole transaction had taken less than ten minutes. Carmichael, a second-level executive at Normandy Trust, prided himself both on his good business sense and his ability to come quickly to a firm decision.

Fifteen minutes later, his car deposited him at the front entrance to their totally detached self-powered suburban home in the fashionable Westley subdivision. The car obediently took itself around back to the garage, while Carmichael stood in the scanner field until the door opened. Clyde, the robutler, came scuttling hastily up, took his hat and cloak, and handed him a Martini.

Carmichael beamed appreciatively. "Well done, thou good and faithful servant!"

He took a healthy sip and headed toward the living room

164

to greet his wife, son and daughter. Pleasant gin-induced warmth filtered through him. The robutler was ancient and due for replacement as soon as the budget could stand the charge, but Carmichael realized he would miss the clanking old heap.

"You're late, dear," Ethel Carmichael said as he appeared. "Dinner's been ready for ten minutes. Jemima's so annoyed her cathodes are clicking."

"Jemima's cathodes fail to interest me," Carmichael said evenly. "Good evening, dear. Myra. Joey. I'm late because I stopped off at Marhew's on my way home."

His son blinked. "The robot place, Dad?"

"Precisely. I brought a '61 roboservitor to replace old Jemima and her spluttering cathodes. The new model has," Carmichael added, eyeing his son's adolescent bulkiness and the rather-more-than-ample figures of his wife and daughter, "some very special attachments."

They dined well that night, on Jemima's favorite Tuesday dinner menu—shrimp cocktail, fumet of gumbo chervil, breast of chicken with creamed potatoes and aparagus, delicious plum tarts for dessert, and coffee. Carmichael felt pleasantly bloated when he had finished, and gestured to Clyde for a snifter of his favorite afterdinner digestive aid, VSOP Cognac. He leaned back, warm, replete, able easily to ignore the blustery November winds outside.

A pleasing electroluminescence suffused the dining room with pink—this year, the experts thought pink improved digestion—and the heating filaments embedded in the wall glowed cozily as they delivered the BTUs. This was the hour for relaxation in the Carmichael household.

"Dad," Joey began hesitantly, "about that canoe trip next weekend—"

Carmichael folded his hands across his stomach and nodded. "You can go, I suppose. Only be careful. If I find out you didn't use the equilibriator this time—"

165

The door chime sounded. Carmichael lifted an eyebrow and swiveled in his chair.

"Who is it, Clyde?"

"He gives his name as Robinson, sir. Of Robinson Robotics, he said. He had a bulky package to deliver."

"It must be that new robocook, Father!" Myra Carmichael exclaimed.

"I guess it is. Show him in, Clyde."

Robinson turned out to be a red-faced, efficient-looking little man in greasy green overalls and a plaid pullover-coat, who looked disapprovingly at the robutler and strode into the Carmichael living room.

He was followed by a lumbering object about seven feet high, mounted on a pair of rolltreads and swathed completely in quilted rags.

"Got him all wrapped up against the cold, Mr. Carmichael. Lot of delicate circuitry in that job. You ought to be proud of him."

"Clyde, help Mr. Robinson unpack the new robocook," Carmichael said.

"That's okay—I can manage it. And it's *not* a robocook, by the way. It's called a roboservitor now. Fancy price, fancy name."

Carmichael heard his wife mutter, "Sam, how much—"

He scowled at her. "Very reasonable, Ethel. Don't worry so much."

He stepped back to admire the roboservitor as it emerged from the quilted swadling. It was big, all right, with a massive barrel of a chest—robotic controls are always housed in the chest, not in the relatively tiny head—and a gleaming mirror-keen finish that accented its sleekness and newness. Carmichael felt the satisfying glow of pride in ownership. Somehow it seemed to him that he had done something noble and lordly in buying this magnificent robot.

Robinson finished the unpacking job and, standing on

166

tiptoes, opened the robot's chest panel. He unclipped a thick instruction manual and handed it to Carmichael, who stared at the tome uneasily.

"Don't fret about that, Mr. Carmichael. This robot's no trouble to handle. The book's just part of the trimming. Come here a minute."

Carmichael peered into the robot's innards. Pointing, Robinson said, "Here's the recipe bank—biggest, and best ever designed. Of course it's possible to tape in any of your favourite family recipes, if they're not already there. Just hook up your old robocook to the integrator circuit and feed 'em in. I'll take care of that before I leave."

"And what about the—ah—special features?"

"The reducing monitors, you mean? Right over here. See? You just tape in the names of the members of the family and their present and desired weights, and the robosevitor takes care of the rest. Computes caloric intake, adjusts menus, and everything else."

Carmichael grinned at his wife. "Told you I was going to do something about our weight, Ethel. No more dieting for you, Myra—the robot does all the work." Catching a sour look on his son's face, he added, "And you're not so lean yourself, Buster."

"I don't think there'll be any trouble," Robinson said buoyantly. "But if there is, just buzz for me. I handle service and delivery for Marhew Stores in this area."

"Right."

"Now if you'll get me your obsolete robocook, I'll transfer the family recipes before I cart it away on the trade-in-deal."

There was a momentary tingle of nostalgia and regret when Robinson left, half an hour later, taking old Jemima with him. Carmichael had almost come to think of the battered '43 Madison as a member of the family. After all, he had bought her sixteen years before, only a couple of years after his marriage.

But she—*it,* he corrected in annoyance—was only a robot, and robots became obsolete. Besides, Jemima probably suffered all the aches and pains of a robot's old age and would .be happier dismantled. Carmichael blotted Jemima from his mind.

The four of them spent most of the rest of that evening discovering things about their new roboservitor. Carmichael drew up a table of their weights (himself, 192; Ethel, 145; Myra, 139; Joey, 189) and the amount they proposed to weigh in three months' time (himself, 180; Ethel, 125; Myra, 120; Joey, 175). Carmichael then let his son, who prided himself on his knowledge of practical robotics, integrate the figures and feed them to the robot's programing bank.

"You wish this schedule to take effect immediately?" the roboservitor queried in a deep, mellow bass.

Startled, Carmichael said, "T-tomorrow morning, at breakfast. We might as well start right away."

"He speaks well, doesn't he?" Ethel asked.

"He sure does," Joey said. "Jemima always stammered and squeaked, and all she could say was, 'Dinner is serrved' and 'Be careful, sirr, the soup plate is verry warrm.' "

Carmichael smiled. He noticed his daughter admiring the robot's bulky frame and sleek bronze limbs, and thought resignedly that a seventeen-year-old girl could find the strangest sorts of love objects. But he was happy to see that they were all evidently pleased with the robot. Even with the discount and the trade-in, it *had* been a little on the costly side.

But it would be worth it.

Carmichael slept soundly and woke early, anticipating the first breakfast under the new regime. He still felt pleased with himself.

Dieting had always been such a nuisance, he thought— but, on the other hand, he had never enjoyed the sensation of an annoying roll of fat pushing outward against his elastobelt. He exercised sporadically, but it did little good, and he never had the initiative to keep a rigorous dieting campaign going for long. Now, though, with the mathematics of reducing done effortlessly for him, all the calculating and cooking being handled by the new robot—now, for the first time since he had been Joey's age, he could look forward to being slim and trim once again.

He dressed, showered and hastily depilated. It was 0730. Breakfast was ready.

Ethel and the children were already at the table when he arrived. Ethel and Myra were munching toast; Joey was peering at a bowl of milkless dry cereal, next to which stood a full glass of milk. Carmichael sat down.

"Your toast, sir," the roboservitor murmured.

Carmichael stared at the single slice. It had already been buttered for him, and the butter had evidently been measured out with a micrometer. The robot proceeded to hand him a cup of black coffee.

He groped for the cream and sugar. They weren't anywhere on the table. The other members of his family were regarding him strangely, and they were curiously, suspiciously silent.

"I like cream and sugar in my coffee," he said to the hovering roboservitor. "Didn't you find that in Jemima's old recipe bank?"

"Of course, sir. But you must learn to drink your coffee without such things, if you wish to lose weight."

Carmichael chuckled. Somehow he had not expected the regimen to be quite like this—quite so, well, Spartan. "Oh, yes. Of course. Ah—are the eggs ready yet?" He considered a day incomplete unless he began it with soft-boiled eggs.

"Sorry, no sir. On Mondays, Wednesdays and Fridays, breakfast is to consist of toast and black coffee only, except for Master Joey, who gets cereal, fruit juice and milk."

"I—see."

Well, he had asked for it. He shrugged and took a bite of the toast. He sipped the coffee; it tasted like river mud, but he tried not to make a face.

Joey seemed to be going about the business of eating his cereal rather oddly, Carmichael noticed next. "Why don't you pour that glass of milk *into* the cereal?" he asked. "Won't it taste better that way?"

"Sure it will. But Bismarck says I won't get another glass if I do, so I'm eating it this way."

"Bismarck?"

Joey grinned. "It's the name of a famous 19th-Century German dictator. They called him the Iron Chancellor." He jerked his head toward the kitchen, to which the robo-servitor had silently retreated. "Pretty good name for him, eh?"

"No," said Carmichael. "It's silly."

"It has a certain ring of truth, though," Ethel remarked.

Carmichael did not reply. He finished his toast and coffee somewhat glumly and signaled Clyde to get the car out of the garage. He felt depressed—dieting didn't seem to be so effortless after all, even with the new robot.

As he walked toward the door, the robot glided around him and handed him a small printed slip of paper. Carmichael stared at it. It said:

FRUIT JUICE

LETTUCE & TOMATO SALAD

(ONE) HARD-BOILED EGG

BLACK COFFEE

"What is this thing?"

"You are the only member of this family group who will not be eating three meals a day under my personal supervision. This is your luncheon menu. Please adhere to it," the robot said smoothly.

170

Repressing a sputter, Carmichael said, "Yes—yes. Of course."

He pocketed the menu and made his way uncertainly to the waiting car.

He was faithful to the robot's orders at lunchtime that day; even though he was beginning to develop resistance to the idea that had seemed so appealing only the night before, he was willing, at least, to give it a try.

But something prompted him to stay away from the restaurant where Normandy Trust employees usually lunched, and where there were human waiters to smirk at him and fellow executives to ask prying questions.

He ate instead at a cheap robocafeteria two blocks to the north. He slipped in surreptitiously with his collar turned up, punched out his order (it cost him less than a credit altogether) and wolfed it down. He still felt hungry when he was finished, but he compelled himself to return loyally to the office.

He wondered how long he was going to be able to keep up this iron self-control. Not very long, he realized dolefully. And if anyone from the company caught him eating at a robocafetcria, he'd be a laughing stock. Someone of executive status just *didn't* eat lunch by himself in mechanized cafeterias.

By the time he had finished his day's work, his stomach felt knotted and pleated. His hand was shaky as he punched out his destination on the car's autopanel, and he was thankful that it took less than an hour to get home from the office. Soon, he thought, he'd be tasting food again. Soon. Soon. He switched on the roof-mounted video, leaned back at the recliner and tried to relax as the car bore him homeward.

He was in for a surprise, though, when he stepped through the safety field into his home. Clyde was waiting as always, and, as always, took his hat and cloak. And, as

171

always, Carmichael reached out for the cocktail that Clyde prepared nightly to welcome him home.

There was no cocktail.

"Are we out of gin, Clyde?"

"No, sir."

"How come no drink, then?"

The robot's rubberized metallic features seemed to droop. "Because, sir, a Martini's caloric content is inordinately high. Gin is rated at a hundred calories per ounce and—"

"Oh, no. You too!"

"Pardon, sir. The new roboservitor has altered my responsive circuits to comply with the regulations now in force in this household."

Carmichael felt his fingers starting to tremble. "Clyde, you've been my butler for almost twenty years."

"Yes, sir."

"You always make my drinks for me. You mix the best Martinis in the Western Hemisphere."

"Thank you, sir."

"And you're going to mix one for me right now! That's a direct order!"

"Sir! I—" The robutler staggered wildly and nearly careened into Carmichael. It seemed to have lost all control over its gyro-balance; it clutched agonizedly at its chest panel and started to sag.

Hastily, Carmichael barked, "Order countermanded! Clyde, are you all right?"

Slowly, and with a creak, the robot straightened up. It looked dangerously close to an overload. "Your direct order set up a first-level conflict in me, sir," Clyde whispered faintly. "I—came close to burning out just then, sir. May—may I be excused?"

"Of course. Sorry, Clyde." Carmichael balled his fists. There was such a thing as going too far! The roboservitor —Bismarck—had obviously placed on Clyde a flat prohi-

172

bition against serving liquor to him. Reducing or no reducing, there were *limits*.

Carmichael strode angrily toward the kitchen.

His wife met him halfway. "I didn't hear you come in, Sam. I want to talk to you about—"

"Later. Where's that robot?"

"In the kitchen, I imagine. It's almost dinnertime."

He brushed past her and swept on into the kitchen, where Bismarck was moving efficiently from electrostove to magnetic worktable. The robot swiveled as Carmichael entered.

"Did you have a good day, sir?"

"No! I'm hungry! "

"The first days of a diet are always the most difficult Mr. Carmichael. But your body will adjust to the reduction in food intake before long."

"I'm sure of that. But what's this business of tinkering with Clyde?"

"The butler insisted on preparing an alcoholic drink for you. I was forced to adjust his programing. From now on, sir, you may indulge in cocktails on Tuesdays, Thursdays, and Saturdays. I beg to be excused from further discussion now, sir. The meal is almost ready."

Poor Clyde! Carmichael thought. *And poor me!* He gnashed his teeth impotently a few times, then gave up and turned away from the glistening, overbearing roboservitor. A light gleamed on the side of the robot's head, indicating that he had shut off his audio circuits and was totally engaged in his task.

Dinner consisted of steak and peas, followed by black coffee. The steak was rare; Carmichael preferred it well done. But Bismarck—the name was beginning to take hold —had had all the latest dietetic theories taped into him, and rare meat it was.

After the robot had cleared the table and tidied up the

173

kitchen, it retired to its storage place in the basement, which gave the Carmichael family a chance to speak openly to each other for the first time that evening.

"Lord! " Ethel snorted. "Sam, I don't object to losing weight, but if we're going to be *tyrannized* in our own home—"

"Mom's right," Joey put in. "It doesn't seem fair for that thing to feed us whatever it pleases. And I didn't like the way is messed around with Clyde's circuits."

Carmichael spread his hands. "I'm not happy about it either. But we have to give it a try. We can always make readjustments in the programing if it turns out to be necessary."

"But how long are we going to keep this up?" Myra wanted to know. "I had three meals in this house today and I'm starved! "

"Me, too," Joey said. He elbowed himself from his chair and looked around. "Bismarck's downstairs. I'm going to get a slice of lemon pie while the coast is clear."

"No! " Carmichael thundered.

"No?"

"There's no sense in my spending three thousand credits on a dietary robot if you're going to cheat, Joey. I forbid you to have any pie."

"But, Dad, I'm hungry! I'm a growing boy! I'm—"

"You're sixteen years old, and if you grow much more, you won't fit inside the house," Carmichael snapped, looking up at his six-foot-one son.

"Sam, we can't starve the boy," Ethel protested. "If he wants pie, let him have some. You're carrying this reduction fetish too far."

Carmichael considered that. Perhaps, he thought, I *am* being a little over severe. And the thought of lemon pie was a tempting one. He was pretty hungry himself.

"All right," he said with feigned reluctance. "I guess a

174

bit of pie won't wreck the plan. In fact, I suppose I'll have some myself. Joey, why don't you—"

"Begging your pardon," a purring voice said behind him. Carmichael jumped half an inch. It was the robot, Bismarck. "It would be most unfortunate if you were to have pie now, Mr. Carmichael. My calculations are very precise."

Carmichael saw the angry gleam in his son's eye, but the robot seemed extraordinarily big at that moment, and it happened to stand between him and the kitchen.

He sighed weakly. "Let's forget the lemon pie, Joey."

After two full days of the Bismarckian diet, Carmichael discovered that his inner resources of will power were beginning to crumble. On the third day he tossed away the printed lunchtime diet and went out irresponsibly with MacDougal and Hennessey for a six-course lunch, complete with cocktails. It seemed to him that he hadn't tasted real food since the robot arrived.

That night, he was able to tolerate the seven-hundred-calorie dinner without any inward grumblings, being still well lined with lunch. But Ethel and Myra and Joey were increasingly irritable. It seemed that the robot had usurped Ethel's job of handling the daily marketing and had stocked in nothing but a huge supply of healthy low-calorie foods. The larder now bulged with wheat germ, protein bread, irrigated salmon, and other hitherto unfamiliar items. Myra had taken up biting her nails; Joey's mood was one of black sullen brooding, and Carmichael knew how that could lead to trouble quickly with a sixteen-year-old.

After the meager dinner, he ordered Bismarck to go to the basement and stay there until summoned.

The robot said, "I must advise you, sir, that I will detect indulgence in any forbidden foods in my absence and adjust for it in the next meals."

"You have my word," Carmichael said, thinking it was

175

indeed queer to have to pledge on your honour to your own robot. He waited until the massive servitor had vanished below; then he turned to Joey and said, "Get the instruction manual, boy."

Joey grinned in understanding. Ethel said, "Sam, what are you going to do?"

Carmichael patted his shrunken waistline. "I'm going to take a can opener to that creature and adjust his programing. He's overdoing this diet business. Joey, have you found the instructions on how to reprogram the robot?"

"Page 167. I'll get the tool kit, Dad."

"Right." Carmichael turned to the robutler, who was standing by dumbly, in his usual forward-stooping posture of expectancy. "Clyde, go down below and tell Bismarck we want him right away."

Moments later, the two robots appeared. Carmichael said to the roboservitor, "I'm afraid it's necessary for us to change your program. We've overestimated our capacity for losing weight."

"I beg you to reconsider, sir. Extra weight is harmful to every vital organ in the body. I plead with you to maintain my scheduling unaltered."

"I'd rather cut my own throat. Joey, inactivate him and do your stuff."

Grinning fiercely, the boy stepped forward and pressed the stud that opened the robot's ribcage. A frightening assortment of gears, cams and translucent cables became visible inside the robot. With a small wrench in one hand and the open instruction book in the other, Joey prepared to make the necessary changes, while Carmichael held his breath and a pall of silence descended on the living room. Even old Clyde leaned forward to have a better view.

Joey muttered, "Lever F2, with the yellow indicia, is to be advanced one notch . . . umm. Now twist Dial B9 to the left, thereby opening the taping compartment and—oops! "

Carmichael heard the clang of a wrench and saw the bright flare of sparks; Joey leaped back, cursing with surprisingly mature skill. Ethel and Myra gasped simultaneously.

"What happened?" four voices—Clyde's coming in last demanded.

"Dropped the damn wrench," Joey said. "I guess I shorted out something in there."

The robot's eyes were whirling satanically and its voice box was emitting an awesome twelve-cycle rumble. The great metal creature stood stiffly in the middle of the living room; with brusque gestures of its big hands, it slammed shut the open chest plates.

"We'd better call Mr. Robinson," Ethel said worriedly. "A short-circuited robot is likely to explode, or worse."

"We should have called Robinson in the first place," Carmichael murmured bitterly. "It's my fault for letting Joey tinker with an expensive and delicate mechanism like that. Myra, get me the card Mr. Robinson left."

"Gee, Dad, this is the first time I've ever had anything like that go wrong," Joey insisted. "I didn't know—"

"You're darned right you didn't know." Carmichael took the card from his daughter and started toward the phone. "I hope we can reach him at this hour. If we can't—"

Suddenly Carmichael felt cold fingers prying the card from his hand. He was so startled he relinquished it without a struggle. He watched as Bismarck efficiently ripped it into little fragments and shoved them into a wall disposal unit.

The robot said. "There will be no further meddling with my program tapes." Its voice was deep and strangely harsh.

"What—"

"Mr. Carmichael, today you violated the program I set down for you. My perceptors reveal that you consumed an

177

amount far in excess of your daily lunchtime requirement."

"Sam, what—"

"Quiet, Ethel. Bismarck, I order you to shut yourself off at once.'

"My apologies, sir. I cannot serve you if I am shut off."

"I don't *want* you to serve me. You're out of order. I want you to remain still until I can phone the repairman and get him to service you."

Then he remembered the card that had gone into the disposal unit. He felt a faint tremor of apprehension.

"You took Robinson's card and destroyed it."

"Further alteration of my circuits would be detrimental to the Carmichael family," said the robot. "I cannot permit you to summon the repairman."

"Don't get him angry, Dad," Joey warned. "I'll call the police. I'll be back in—"

"You will remain within this house," the robot said. Moving with impressive speed on its oiled treads, it crossed the room, blocking the door, and reached far above its head to activate the impassable privacy field that protected the house. Carmichael watched, aghast, as the inexorable robotic fingers twisted and manipulated the field controls.

"I have now reversed the polarity of the house privacy field," the robot announced. "Since you are obviously not to be trusted to keep to the diet I prescribe, I cannot allow you to leave the premises. You will remain within and continue to obey my beneficial advice."

Calmly, he uprooted the telephone. Next, the windows were opaqued and the stud broken off. Finally, the robot seized the instruction book from Joey's numbed hands and shoved it into the disposal unit.

"Breakfast will be served at the usual time," Bismarck said mildly. "For optimum purposes of health, you are all

178

to be asleep by 2300 hours. I shall leave you now, until morning. Good night."

Carmichael did not sleep well that night, nor did he eat well the next day. He awoke late, for one thing—well past nine. He discovered that someone, obviously Bismarck, had neatly canceled out the impulses from the housebrain that woke him at seven each morning.

The breakfast menu was toast and black coffee. Carmichael ate disgruntedly, not speaking, indicating by brusque scowls that he did not want to be spoken to. After the miserable meal had been cleared away, he surreptitiously tiptoed to the front door in his dressing gown and darted a hand toward the handle.

The door refused to budge. He pushed until sweat dribbled down his face. He heard Ethel whisper warningly, "*Sam—*" and a moment later cool metallic fingers gently disengaged him from the door.

Bismarck said, "I beg your pardon, sir. The door will not open. I explained this last night.'

Carmichael gazed sourly at the gimmicked control box of the privacy field. The robot had them utterly hemmed in. The reversed privacy field made it impossible for them to leave the house; it cast a sphere of force around the entire detached dwelling. In theory, the field could be penetrated from outside, but nobody was likely to come calling without an invitation. Not here in Westley. It wasn't one of those neighborly subdivisions where everybody knew everybody else. Carmichael had picked it for that reason.

"Damn you," he growled, "you can't hold us *prisoners* in here! "

"My intent is only to help you," said the robot, in a mechanical yet dedicated voice. "My function is to supervise your diet. Since you will not obey willingly, obedience must be enforced—for your own good."

Carmichael scowled and walked away. The worst part of it was that the roboservitor sounded so *sincere!*

179

Trapped. The phone connection was severed. The windows were darkened. Somehow, Joey's attempt at repairs had resulted in a short circuit of the robot's obedience filters, and had also exaggeratedly stimulated its sense of function. Now Bismarck was determined to make them lose weight if it had to kill them to do so.

And that seemed very likely.

Blockaded, the Carmichael family met in a huddled little group to whisper plans for a counterattack. Clyde stood watch, but the robutler seemed to be in a state of general shock since the demonstration of the servitor-robot's independent capacity for action, and Carmichael now regarded him as undependable.

"He's got the kitchen walled off with some kind of electronic-based force web," Joey said. "He must have built it during the night. I tried to sneak in and scrounge some food, and got nothing but a flat nose for trying."

"I know," Carmichael said sadly. "He built the same sort of doohickey around the bar. Three hundred credits of good booze in there and I can't even grab the handle! "

"This is no time to worry about drinking," Ethel said morosely. "We'll be skeletons any day."

"It isn't *that* bad, Mom! " Joey said.

"Yes, it is! " cried Myra. "I've lost five pounds in four days! "

"Is that so terrible?"

"I'm wasting away," she sobbed. "My figure—it's vanishing! And—"

"Quiet," Carmichael whispered. "Bismarck's coming! "

The robot emerged from the kitchen, passing through the force barrier as if it had been a cobweb. It seemed to have effect on humans only, Carmichael thought. "Lunch will be served in eight minutes," it said obsequiously, and returned to its lair.

Carmichael glanced at his watch. The time was 1230

hours. "Probably down at the office they're wondering where I am," he said. "I haven't missed a day's work in years."

"They won't care," Ethel said. "An executive isn't required to account for every day off he takes, you know."

"But they'll worry after three or four days, won't they?" Myra asked. "Maybe they'll try to phone—or even send a rescue mission!"

From the kitchen, Bismarck said coldly, "There will be no danger of that. While you slept this morning, I notified your place of employment that you were resigning."

Carmichael gasped. Then, recovering, he said: "You're lying! The phone's cut off—and you never would have risked leaving the house, even if we *were* asleep!"

"I communicated with them via a microwave generator I constructed with the aid of your son's reference books last night," Bismarck replied. "Clyde reluctantly supplied me with the number. I also phoned your bank and instructed them to handle for you all such matters as tax payments, investment decisions, etc. To forestall difficulties, let me add that a force web will prevent access on your part to the electronic equipment in the basement. I will be able to conduct such communication with the outside world as will be necessary for your welfare, Mr. Carmichael. You need have no worries on that score."

"No," Carmichael echoed hollowly. "No worries."

He turned to Joey. "We've got to get out of here. Are you sure there's no way of disconnecting the privacy field?"

"He's got one of his force fields rigged around the control box. I can't even get near the thing."

"If only we had an iceman, or an oilman, the way the oldtime houses did," Ethel said bitterly. "He'd show up and come inside and probably he'd know how to shut the field off. But not *here*. Oh, no. We've got a shiny chrome-plated cryostat in the basement that dishes out lots of

181

liquid helium to run the fancy cryotronic super-cooled power plant that gives us heat and light, and we have enough food in the freezer to last for at least a decade or two, and so we can live like this for years, a neat little self-contained island in the middle of civilization, with nobody bothering us, nobody wondering about us, and Sam Carmichael's pet robot to feed us whenever and as little as it pleases—"

There was a cutting edge to her voice that was dangerously close to hysteria.

"Ethel, please," said Carmichael.

"Please what? Please keep quiet? Please stay calm? Sam, we're *prisoners* in here! "

"I know. You don't have to raise your voice."

"Maybe if I do, someone will hear us and come and get us out," she replied more coolly.

"It's four hundred feet to the next home, dear. And in the seven years we've lived here, we've had about two visits from our neighbors. We paid a stiff price for seclusion and now we're paying a stiffer one. But please keep under control, Ethel."

"Don't worry, Mom. I'll figure a way out of this," Joey said reassuringly.

In one corner of the living room, Myra was sobbing quietly to herself, blotching her makeup. Carmichael felt a faintly claustrophobic quiver. The house was big, three levels and twelve rooms, but even so he could get tired of it very quickly.

"Luncheon is served," the roboservitor announced in booming tones.

And tired of lettuce-and-tomato lunches, too, Carmichael added silently, as he shepherded his family toward the dining room for their meager midday meal.

"You have to do *something* about this, Sam," Ethel Carmichael said on the third day of their imprisonment.

182

He glared at her. "Have to, eh? And just what am I supposed to do?"

"Daddy, don't get excited," Myra said.

He whirled on her. "Don't tell me what I should or shouldn't do! "

"She can't help it, dear. We're all a little overwrought. After all, cooped up here—"

"I know. Like lambs in a pen," he finished acidly. "Except that we're not being fattened for slaughter. We're—we're being *thinned*, and for our own alleged good! "

Carmichael subsided gloomily. Toast-and-black-coffee, lettuce-and-tomato, rare-steak-and-peas. Bismarck's channels seemed to have frozen permanently at that daily menu.

But what could he do?

Contact with the outside world was impossible. The robot had erected a bastion in the basement from which he conducted such little business with the world as the Carmichael family had. Generally, they were self-sufficient. And Bismarck's force fields insured the impossibility of any attempts to disconnect the outer sheath, break into the basement, or even get at the food supply or the liquor. It was all very neat, and the four of them were fast approaching a state of starvation.

"Sam?"

He lifted his head wearily. "What is it, Ethel?"

"Myra had an idea before. Tell him, Myra."

"Oh, it would never work," Myra said demurely.

"Tell *him!*"

"Well—Dad, you *could* try to turn Bismarck off."

"Huh?" Carmichael grunted.

"I mean if you or Joey could distract him somehow, then Joey or you could open him up again and—"

"No," Carmichael snapped. "That thing's seven feet tall and weighs three hundred pounds. If you think *I'm* going to wrestle with it—"

"We could let Clyde try," Ethel suggested.

Carmichael shook his head vehemently. "The carnage would be frightful."

Joey said, "Dad, it may be our only hope."

"You too?" Carmichael asked.

He took a deep breath. He felt himself speared by two deadly feminine glances, and he knew there was no hope but to try it. Resignedly, he pushed himself to his feet and said, "Okay. Clyde, go call Bismarck. Joey, I'll try to hang onto his arms while you open up his chest. Yank anything you can."

"Be careful," Ethel warned. "If there's an explosion—"

"If there's an explosion, we're all free," Carmichael said testily. He turned to see the broad figure of the roboservitor standing at the entrance to the living room.

"May I be of service, sir?"

"You may," Carmichael said. "We're having a little debate here and we want your evidence. It's a matter of defannising the poozlestan and—*Joey, open him up!*"

Carmichael grabbed for the robot's arms, trying to hold them without getting hurled across the room, while his son clawed frantically at the stud that opened the robot's innards. Carmichael anticipated immediate destruction—but, to his surprise, he found himself slipping as he tried to grasp the thick arms.

"Dad, it's no use. I—he—"

Carmichael found himself abruptly four feet off the ground. He heard Ethel and Myra scream and Clyde's, "*Do* be careful, sir."

Bismarck was carrying them across the room, gently, cradling him in one giant arm and Joey in the other. It set them down on the couch and stood back.

"Such an attempt is highly dangerous," Bismarck said reprovingly. "It puts me in danger of harming you physically. Please avoid any such acts in the future."

184

Carmichael stared broodingly at his son. "Did you have the same trouble I did?"

Joey nodded. "I couldn't get within an inch of his skin. It stands to reason, though. He's built one of those damned force screens around *himself*, too! "

Carmichael groaned. He did not look at his wife and his children. Physical attack on Bismarck was now out of the question. He began to feel as if he had been condemned to life imprisonment—and that his stay in durance vile would not be extremely prolonged.

In the upstairs bathroom, six days after the beginning of the blockade, Sam Carmichael stared at his haggard fleshless face in the mirror before wearily climbing on the scale.

He weighed 180.

He had lost twelve pounds in less than two weeks. He was fast becoming a quivering wreck.

A thought occurred to him as he stared at the wavering needle on the scale, and sudden elation spread over him. He dashed downstairs. Ethel was doggedly crocheting in the living room; Joey and Myra were playing cards grimly, desperately now, after six solid days of gin rummy and honeymoon bridge.

"Where's that robot?" Carmichael roared. "Come out here! "

"In the kitchen," Ethel said tonelessly.

"Bismarck! Bismarck! " Carmichael roared. "Come out here! "

The robot appeared. "How may I serve you sir?"

"Damn you, scan me with your superpower receptors and tell me how much I weigh! "

After a pause, the robot said gravely, "One hundred seventy-nine pounds eleven ounces, Mr. Carmichael."

"Yes! Yes! And the original program I had taped into you was supposed to reduce me from 192 to 180," Carmichael crowed triumphantly. "So I'm finished with you, as long as I don't gain any more weight. And so are the rest of us, I'll bet. Ethel! Myra! Joey! Upstairs and weigh yourselves!"

But the robot regarded him with a doleful glare and said, "Sir, I find no record within me of any limitation on your reduction of weight."

"What?"

"I have checked my tapes fully. I have a record of an order causing weight reduction, but that tape does not appear to specify a *terminus ad quem.*"

Carmichael exhaled and took three staggering steps backward. His legs wobbled; he felt Joey supporting him. He mumbled, "But I thought—I'm sure we did—I *know* we instructed you—"

Hunger gnawed at his flesh. Joey said softly, "Dad, probably that part of his tape was erased when he short-circuited."

"Oh," Carmichael said numbly.

He tottered into the living room and collapsed heavily in what had once been his favorite armchair. It wasn't any more. The entire house had become odious to him. He longed to see the sunlight again, to see trees and grass, even to see that excrescence of an ultramodern house that the left-hand neighbors had erected.

But now that would be impossible. He had hoped, for a few minutes at least, that the robot would release them from dietary bondage when the original goal was shown to be accomplished. Evidently that was to be denied him. He giggled, then began to laugh.

"What's so funny, dear?" Ethel asked. She had lost her earlier tendencies to hysteria, and after long days of complex crocheting now regarded the universe with quiet resignation.

"Funny? The fact that I weigh 180 now. I'm lean, trim, fit as a fiddle. Next month I'll weigh 170. Then 160. Then finally about 88 pounds or so. We'll all shrivel up. Bismarck will starve us to death."

"Don't worry, Dad. We're going to get out of this."

Somehow Joey's brash boyish confidence sounded forced now. Carmichael shook his head. "We won't. We'll never get out. And Bismarck's going to reduce us *ad infinitum*. He's got no *terminus ad quem!*"

"What's he saying?" Myra asked.

"It's Latin," Joey explained. "But listen, Dad—I have an idea that I think will work." He lowered his voice. "I'm going to try to adjust Clyde, see? If I can get a sort of multiphase vibrating effect in his neural pathway, maybe I can slip him through the reversed privacy field. He can go get help, find someone who can shut the field off. There's an article on multiphase generators in last month's *Popular Electromagnetics* and it's in my room upstairs. I—"

His voice died away. Carmichael, who had been listening with the air of a condemned man hearing his reprieve, said impatiently, "Well? Go on. Tell me more."

"Didn't you hear that, Dad?"

"Hear what?"

"The front door. I thought I heard it open just now."

"We're all cracking up," Carmichael said dully. He cursed the salesman at Marhew, he cursed the inventor of cryotronic robots, he cursed the day he had first felt ashamed of good old Jemima and resolved to replace her with a new model.

"I hope I'm not intruding, Mr. Carmichael," a new voice said apologetically.

Carmichael blinked and looked up. A wiry, ruddy-cheeked figure in a heavy peajacket had materialized in the middle of the living room. He was clutching a green metal toolbox in one gloved hand. He was Robinson, the robot repairman.

Carmichael asked hoarsely, "How did *you* get in?"

"Through the front door. I could see a light on inside,

but nobody answered the doorbell when I rang, so I stepped in. Your doorbell's out of order. I thought I'd tell you. I know it's rude—"

"Don't apologize," Carmichael muttered. "We're delighted to see you."

"I was in the neighborhood, you see, and I figured I'd drop in and see how things were working out with your new robot," Robinson said.

Carmichael told him crisply and precisely and quickly. "So we've been prisoners in here for six days," he finished. "And your robot is gradually starving us to death. We can't hold out much longer."

The smile abruptly left Robinson's cheery face. "I *thought* you all looked rather unhealthy. Oh, damn, now there'll be an investigation and all kinds of trouble. But at least I can end your imprisonment."

He opened his toolbox and selected a tubular instrument eight inches long, with a glass bulb at one end and a trigger attachment at the other. "Force-field damper," he explained. He pointed it at the control box of the privacy field and nodded in satisfaction. "There. Great little gadget. That neutralizes the effects of what the robot did and you're no longer blockaded. And now, if you'll produce the robot—"

Carmichael sent Clyde off to get Bismarck. The robutler returned a few moments later, followed by the looming roboservitor. Robinson grinned gaily, pointed the neutralizer at Bismarck and squeezed. The robot froze in mid-glide, emitting a brief squeak.

"There. That should immoblize him. Let's have a look in that chassis now."

The repairman quickly opened Bismarck's chest and, producing a pocket flash, peered around in the complex interior of the servomechanism, making occasional clucking inaudible comments.

Overwhelmed with relief, Carmichael shakily made his

way to a seat. Free! Free at last! His mouth watered at the thought of the meals he was going to have in the next few days. Potatoes and Martinis and warm buttered rolls and all the other forbidden foods!

"Fascinating," Robinson said, half to himself. "The obedience filters are completely shorted out, and the purpose nodes were somehow soldered together by the momentary high-voltage arc. I've never seen anything quite like this, you know."

"Neither had we," Carmichael said hollowly.

"Really, though—this is an utterly new breakthrough in robotic science! If we can reproduce this effect, it means we can build self-willed robots—and think of what *that* means to science! "

"We know already," Ethel said.

"I'd love to watch what happens when the power source is operating," Robinson went on. "For instance, is that feedback loop really negative or—"

"No! " five voices shrieked at once—with Clyde, as usual, coming in last.

It was too late. The entire event had taken no more than a tenth of a second. Robinson had squeezed his neutralizer trigger again, activating Bismarck—and in one quick swoop the roboservitor seized neutralizer and toolbox from the stunned repairman, activated the privacy field once again, and exultantly crushed the fragile neutralizer between two mighty fingers.

Robinson stammered, "but—but—"

"This attempt at interfering with the well-being of the Carmichael family was ill-advised," Bismarck said severely. He peered into the toolbox, found a second neutralizer and neatly reduced it to junk. He clanged shut his chest plates.

Robinson turned and streaked for the door, forgetting the reactivated privacy field. He bounced back hard, spinning wildly around. Carmichael rose from his seat just in time to catch him.

There was a panicky, trapped look on the repairman's face. Carmichael was no longer able to share the emotion; inwardly he was numb, totally resigned, not minded for further struggle.

"He—he moved so *fast*! " Robinson burst out.

"He did indeed," Carmichael said tranquilly. He patted his hollow stomach and sighed gently. "Luckily, we have an unoccupied guest bedroom for you, Mr. Robinson. Welcome to our happy little home. I hope you like toast and black coffee for breakfast."

James Clavell
TAI-PAN

Now only 10/6
704 Pages

In this turbulent, panoramic novel of the
founding of Hong Kong, James Clavell, author of
KING RAT, narrates the saga of how one
man, with majestic vision, ruthless will and
ingenious grasp of command, guides the development
of a colony destined to influence the course
of history. It is a masterful re-creation
of a momentous epoch in the history
of the British Empire.

J.A.C. Brown
Pears Medical
Encyclopaedia

7/6

555 Pages

This newly revised edition of a famous household
reference work is as interesting as a novel
and as informative as its sister volume,
PEARS CYCLOPAEDIA. It covers the wide range
of Medical Matters, relates modern medicine to its
social background and talks sheer good
sense on many controversial and taboo topics.

The new edition includes many entries dealing
with contemporary problems. The Pill is here,
so is E.C.T., "Fringe Medicine", the population
explosion, lung cancer, tranquilisers and drug
addiction. But perhaps its most valuable
quality is its commonsense approach to everyday
anxieties about health.